A BOOK

Sara Maitland won the Somerset Maugham Award
with her first novel, *Daughter of Jerusalem*,
published in 1978. Her second, *Virgin Territory*,
was published to much acclaim in 1984. Most
recently she scored enormous critical success with
her biography of Vesta Tilley for the Virago
Pioneers series, and also co-published with
Michelene Wandor the satirical epistolary novel
Arky Types. Sara Maitland has contributed to a
number of anthologies and reviewed extensively for
a wide variety of newspapers and magazines. She
lives in a Gothic vicarage in east London with her
husband, an Anglican priest, and her two children.

Also by Sara Maitland

NOVELS
Daughter of Jerusalem
Virgin Territory
Arky Types (with Michelene Wandor)*

SHORT STORIES
Telling Tales
Weddings and Funerals
(with Aileen Latourette)

NON-FICTION
A Map of the New Country
Vesta Tilley

*available from Methuen

A BOOK OF SPELLS

Sara Maitland

A Methuen Paperback

A Methuen Paperback

A BOOK OF SPELLS

First published in Great Britain 1987
by Michael Joseph Ltd
This edition published 1988
by Methuen London
81 Fulham Road, London SW3 6RB
This collection © Sara Maitland 1987

Printed and bound in Great Britain by
Richard Clay Ltd, Bungay, Suffolk

British Library Cataloguing in Publication Data

Maitland, Sara, *1950–*
A book of spells.
I. Title
823'.914[F]

ISBN 0-413-18270-3

'Heart Throb' first appeared in *Passion Fruit*,
Jeanette Winterson (ed.), Pandora, 1986.
'A Fall from Grace' first appeared in *Weddings and Funerals*,
Aileen Latourette and Sara Maitland, Brilliance, 1984.
'The Wicked Stepmother's Lament' first appeared in
More Tales I Tell My Mother, Zoe Fairbairns,
Sara Maitland, Valerie Miner, Michèle Roberts,
Michelene Wandor, Journeyman, 1987.
'Let us now praise unknown women and our mothers
who begat us' first appeared in *Stepping Out*,
Ann Oosthuizen (ed.), 1986.

CONTENTS

— ❧ —

ACKNOWLEDGEMENTS

The word 'spells' means not only magical charms and incantations but also, and more primarily, 'stories', or 'news' – as in the German '*spiel*' or the word Gospel.

There is also another, unrelated, meaning. A 'spell' is also 'a turn of work taken by a person in relief of some other person or persons'. When I started this book I planned it to be a sort of dedicatory volume for my friends with each story specifically acknowledging the gift – of incident, mood, or material – that had initiated the story for me; a way of saying thank you and a way of making explicit my understanding of the social and communal nature of a creative process; I don't 'make things up' in some secret privacy, but receive things, transform things and give things back. However, the book did not work out quite so simply; I realised how much more complicated the whole process was; ideas became amalgamated, inextricably entwined; identifying single moments' special sources proved too complicated. Moreover, the content of some of these stories, and the difficulties that many readers appear to have with the process of fictionalising, seemed to make the naming of names more of a potential embarrassment than a grateful gift.

So I changed my mind. Here instead, in alphabetical order, I thank the people who, in different ways, with or without intention, have helped me make the stories in this book: Peter Daly, Willow Evans, Jo Garcia, Matt Hoffman, Ros Hunt, Adam Lee, Donald Lee, Mildred Lee, Désirée Martin, Mandy Merck, Anne Scheibner, Maggie Scott, Michelene Wandor.

Philosophy is odious and obscure
Both law and physic are for petty wits,
Divinity is basest of the three,
Unpleasant, harsh, contemptible and vile:
'Tis magic, magic that hath ravished me.

Christopher Marlowe, *Dr Faustus*, c. 1588

ANGEL MAKER

❦

Gretel will come through the forest again this afternoon, as she has come so many times before, since that first time.

It is a golden October day; last night I smelled for the first time this year the distant savour of frost – it was still far away in the Northlands, but hunting southwards following the swallows and pushing before it nights of jewel-bright sharpness and days of astonishing radiance – the sky dazzling blue in contrast to the soft mysterious gold yellows and flame reds of the leaves and the ground-cover grass still green, a green that is deeper now than at any time of year – the frail yellow hues of spring and the dusty density of summer both gone, washed away by the September rain. It is quiet in the forest at this time of year, not silent but a gentle, rustly quiet, except when the winds blow. Today it is not windy nor will be before evening when, if I am not too tired by the events of the afternoon, I will call up a wind and dance, crazy, ancient and unseen, along with the dying leaves whose final flourishing will amuse both them and me.

But before that Gretel will come; discerning in her need the cryptic signs of the path through the forest and walking with a firm but cautious stride. Her laced canvas boots will be the same green as the grass and the tufts of her short hair will blend with the extreme oranges and purples of the autumn wood. She has grown into a beautiful woman, as I always knew she would, and

1

though I think her foolish now, that is not my problem but hers. I do not choose, I never have chosen, to make other women's choices my problem; I do not judge and I do not take the consequences of my refusal to judge. That is my privilege and the price that they must pay for my services. She will regret it, or not regret it, as time alone will show, and her daughter one day perhaps will seek me out in some other forest, in some other time. And in the meantime she has grown into a beautiful woman, for those who have eyes to see it.

I am waiting for her in the bright morning, while my winter doves pick seeds around the gingerbread house. Some things do not change and the windows are all still made of spun sugar, as white and clear as glass, but melting sweet. But bubblegum has solved the old problem of keeping the place together and progress is something I have always believed in. She is a grown-up now but still she prefers, as I prefer, the sugar-candy gingerbread to the chromium and steel cleanliness that some others offer. It is warmth and comfort a woman needs at such times, not hard shiny edges – them as want that can go elsewhere and good riddance to bad rubbish I say.

She will come alone this time.

That is something; something gained in so many centuries.

Of course, the first time she came, all neat and pretty in her cotton skirts and tidy pinny, she was so young that she had to bring him with her – Hansel, I mean; they were not old enough to be separated, she could not go out and about without the boy-child. I saw them come through the forest and they seemed like any two little children to me then, tasty enough and milky sweet, and their eyes huge and round under those thick little fringes, lighting with joy at the sight of the sweety sticky house. But I did not recognise her, even though I could not but admire the abandoned greed with which she tucked into the sweet things on offer, licking at my window till the panes melted and ran down her chin in runnels of sweetness.

I called to her in a whisper,

> *Nibble, nibble, nibble mouse,*
> *Who is nibbling at my little house?*

I should have known her from her answer but I had been alone too long. She smiled and sang,

> *The wind, the wind,*
> *The heaven-born wind.*

Ah, but she was a lucky one then, she had not sought me out knowingly, though without needy desire I cannot be found; the desire was there – the need to be comforted for the loss of her mother, the desire to be comforted for the betrayal by her father. She needed no special magic that time, just showing. So I locked him up, and fattened him up, and let her see that she could be without him, that she was strong and wise and could decide for herself. It worked, though I scared her so badly that she thrust me into the oven and burned me to death and went home and told them that I ate little children.

Well, every sane witch fears fire, it would be folly not to. It was my fault, I thought she was so young that I could decide for her. But it is not permitted; she chose him over me and all I could do was help them find their way back to Daddy afterwards. Now I never choose on their behalf. I wait. I wait. As I wait for her now.

I waited that time ten years and several centuries. She came back when she needed to. She came through the forest, a long swirling skirt spreading its Indian patterns around her, her hair long, its tendrils twisting in and out of the sunlight and adorned with ribbons; her feet were bare on the grass; her breasts were full and her hips sinuous. Her lips looked like those of a woman fulfilled, but her eyes like those of a woman betrayed. Betrayed again.

She stood on the edge of the clearing, and that greed had disappeared under an anxiety. She did not even smile to see the gingerbread and sugar cottage. She looked at me as though she hated me.

I smiled a little, and said,

> *Nibble, nibble, nibble mouse.*
> *Who is nibbling at my little house?*

I thought it might remind her and comfort her.
She said, almost reluctantly, 'They say you can help me.'

'Love potions?' I reply. 'Charms for safety at sea? For murrain among cows, and zits on your rival's nose? Eye of newt and toe of dog.'

I know she has not come for these, but I never decide for my women; they must ask me. It is not my problem.

Slowly she leaves the protection of the tall trees and crosses into the sunlight of my clearing; the chickens cheep and the doves coo; I reach up and break a soft piece of gingerbread, sparkly with sugar, off the eave above my head, and hold it out to her. She takes it almost fiercely and chews. There is a pause and then she says, 'I'm pregnant.'

'I know,' I say, and we wait in a long silence while she masticates the cake in her mouth, her long beady ear-rings joggling about. I know she is waiting for me to offer, but I am an old witch woman and I say nothing. The silence lengthens, even the trees seem hushed and the scratching of the birds fades away. I cannot help her if she cannot ask. After a while, I shuffle inside and get on with things. I think what a tough and joyous child she was all those years ago, shrieking and complaining, and I am angry. I do the washing up, trying not to bang the pots too loudly. I heat the oven and spray on the foam oven-cleaner; when I look out through the sugar-spun windows she is still standing in the clearing, her outline wavery and out of focus from the impurities in the sugar.

At length, she comes to the doorway, and looks in.

'Remember?' I ask, but she shakes her head.

I think she does remember, though, because after only a tiny pause she says, 'I want it got rid of.'

'All right,' I say.

'It's against the law,' she mutters; I don't mind being checked out, it seems sensible to me.

'Not my law,' I tell her. 'Your law?'

Suddenly she becomes verbose, 'It's like this, you see, it's not that I don't like babies, it's just that he . . .'

'No,' I say, quite stern. 'Don't tell me, I don't want to know. I won't blame and I won't praise. There is only one reason: you want it. Nothing else. I'm not interested.'

Suddenly she smiles, shy and illuminated. 'OK,' she says, 'let's do it.'

I go to the back of the cottage and fetch the cauldron; I swing it up on to the hook over the fire. I tell her to lie down. I fill the cauldron and start the long spell.

'Will it hurt?' she asks. 'Wait and see,' I answer.

The smoke rises and swirls about the room, and I take her hand and we go together into another place, a dark and magical room where women go to take charge over destiny, over forests and growing time and small birds and sugar-candy windows, because we choose to. It is a place of risk. It is not a good place, but we go, not because we must, but because we will.

Hours later, we come back and it is dark. It is cold and draughty, because the fire has melted the window panes and the night winds are coming in. I wrap her in a quilt stitched of all the good things in the forest and in the tales of childhood, and then although I am tired I melt more sugar and remake my windows.

In the morning I make her a nice cup of tea and give her a sugar bun plucked from beside the bathroom down-drain. While she gets dressed I sew the scarlet flowering pimpernels which have bloomed on her undersheet into the quilt for the next woman. When she comes down I think that she will leave in silence, but at the last moment she turns to me and says, 'Will she be all right, my daughter?'

I should refuse to answer, I should keep my own rules, but it is she, it is Gretel, the little child who came to me in great loss and fear all those years ago, and I love her. So I answer, 'They don't call me the Angel Maker for nothing.'

It takes her a moment or two to work it out; it is, after all, very early in the morning. Suddenly she grins an enormous evil grin, full of dislike of me, of herself, of the world; also full of irony, and joy and freedom and knowledge. She bunches her fingers into a fist and without warning smashes into one of my newly set windows. She takes a huge chunk of sugar in her hand and sucks it voluptuously. Then she turns, crosses the clearing and goes back into the forest. I think I have seen the last of her, and stand recovering my energy from the gentle warmth of the morning sun, but after a few moments she reappears from behind a tree; she waves her sugar-candy shard at me and shouts, 'Sod the bastards, just sod the lot of them. Including Him.' And she goes

5

away leaving me cackling in my clearing, with yet another window to cook. And another long wait.

I waited again. Understand, she came a thousand times; she came a thousand times as the little child with her brother who did not understand her mother's withdrawal, who did not understand her father's betrayal; she came a thousand times as the young woman with some man's child, with her own child in her belly. And yet I still waited for her to come again. I waited in almost perfect patience. I waited until last month, a wet morning after the turn of the moon, and she came again. I knew she would.

During the waiting time, business had changed. Little call now for love potions and cures for the murrain and kettle mending and fire tending and the little spells of yesteryear. They have Dating Agencies and Inoculations and Hire Purchase and Calor Gas: all of which I might say are strong magics, stronger than mine, and cheaper, and more secret. I have always favoured progress. In the end they took even the deep magic; they changed their laws and called mine quackery. I still hold that a woman needs another woman's hand to clasp and a little sugar splinter to suck on when she goes into the dark place and takes control of the spinning of her own destiny; they say she needs hygiene and counselling and medical attention and I say I never lost one who could be saved, and when they were done with me they knew that they had chosen and were responsible for that. I never questioned that they sucked by the wind, the heaven-born wind, and that those who needed me could find me always. But there is always magic business for a self-respecting old witch to live off. I move with the times, I invested in an oxygen-cooled thermos-flask, and went out and charmed the men they needed, and I waited for her to come.

She was thirty-eight now and could not wait much longer. Stupid, though. In the end I had to go to the town and lay down clues. It was breaking my own rules, of course, and I knew it. It was a long time since I had walked on streets which had hard surfaces and bright neon lights; there were fireworks in every puddle, magic fireworks mothered by the brightness of the lights, golden and sparkly in the wind. But though I had gone with intent, when I saw the first of the children I was innocent and delighted. A darling little thing, wrapped not in a blanket but in a sensible progressive snowsuit, her dark eyes poking up over the edge of a red and green padded snowsuit, and bright with the joy of being a wanted child. Her mother, stiff with pride and tiredness, pushed her in a little open wheeled chair, more frail and fairy than any pumpkin carriage.

'Oh, the little angel,' I cried, and fell upon her with an improper kiss. Perhaps we make rules only for the strange and painful pleasure of breaking them. Her mother recognised me, of course, and was appalled. I saw her stiffen with embarrassment and turn aside with a charm to ward off evil. '"Aroint thee, witch",' the rump-fed runnion cried (her girlfriend's to Aleppo gone, mistress of a Channel 4 documentary, but in a sieve I'll thither sail and like a rat without a tail I'll do, I'll do and I'll do) – does she take responsibility for what she does, despite my best efforts? I wonder. But I saw that Gretel was there and her eyes widened and her wonder deepened. I knew that she would come. And she did. And we talked women talk and agreed that today is the day that she must come. I will do for her what she cannot bring herself to do for herself. I ask no questions and make no judgements, that is not my task. I taught her so long ago that she had to find her own strength and draw upon it, so I can scarcely complain if she draws upon mine.

Last night it was cold; riding upon my broomstick I smelled for the first time this year the distant savour of frost – it was still far away in the Northlands, but hunting southwards following the swallows and pushing before it nights of jewel-bright sharpness and days of astonishing radiance – the moon, so round as to spin the whole cosmos, rode out the darkness anchored to the lee of a ragged cloud, frilled and furbelowed in reflected silver.

He is handsome, the miller's wife's dark son, and his father astute and sturdy; they do not take fever, those children, and they grow beside the weir wide-eyed and hopeful, the rushing water stirring something in them that this child of Gretel's will need. Five centuries ago I would have sent her to him in the gloaming time and given her a little magic potion just in the unlikely case that he was unwilling, but I have taught her to stand firmer to her dignity even than that. Five centuries ago I might have burned for it, but I do not think of that. I may be old and ugly, but he is young and beautiful, and flattery will get one anywhere. Just now he loves a handsome piper from the king's castle keep and loves himself enough to love his own sperm and rejoice that he can spread it here and there without having either effort or responsibility. He will do perfectly for Gretel, and he gives me the ingredient of my magic and feels flattered to do so. At home I spin the crawling fluid in my centrifuge: I only make girl babies, but that is my secret, my power, the one thing I do not let my women choose for themselves – I have some professional dignity. Then I return the fluid to the vial and place it in the refrigerating thermos. I boil the cauldron and wait. Gretel will come through the forest again this afternoon, as she has come so many times before, since that first time.

And she comes, discerning in her need the cryptic signs of the path through the forest and walking with a firm but cautious stride. Her laced canvas boots are the same green as the grass and the tufts of her short hair blend with the extreme oranges and purples of the autumn wood. She has grown into a beautiful woman, as I always knew she would, and though I think her foolish now, that is not my problem but hers. She barely greets me, intent on her own journey and needing. I take her hand and lead her inside the cottage; for the first time I do not bother to break off any titbit for her, knowing that she does not really desire anything except the vial and its magic potency.

I give it to her without further ado. The glass twinkles more clearly than my spun-sugar windows, but I pass no comment upon this. I say only, 'Do you know what to do?' I watch as her square strong knuckles close around the magic potion. 'Yes, alas,' she says, and it is a new grin of self-knowing and a deep irony. 'Go in there,' I tell her, and point towards the door of the bedroom. 'The quilt is on the bed. Make yourself at home.' I swear I meant no joke, but she grinned again and said, 'Do you trust me? Don't you want to come too?' Her irony dissolves and she says, like a little child, 'Please come and help me.' And I, clinging to my own rules like a woman who expects to be saved by good conduct, say, 'No.'

8

I go out of the house and into the clearing. The grass is green and bright; only a little way away the trees of the forest flaunt their autumn colouring; when, after the winter, the summer comes again, Gretel will have a little girl child nursing at her breast. It is what she wants and what I have given her. And though I think her foolish, that is not my problem but hers. I do not choose, I have never chosen, to make other women's choices my problem; I do not judge and I do not take the consequences of my refusal to judge. That is my privilege and the price that they must pay for my services. She will regret it, or not regret it, as time alone will show, and her daughter one day perhaps will seek me out in some other forest, in some other time. And in the meantime she has grown into a beautiful woman, for those who have eyes to see it.

I busy myself as best I may about the clearing, and watch my chickens and my doves busy about their autumn work of feeding and preening, content during this resting time to be sufficient unto themselves, neither mating nor brooding. After what seems like a long, long while, I hear a sudden noisy crash and a tinkling shattering noise. A moment later Gretel emerges; the magic vial now empty, the spell used, is crushed into fragments in her left hand, from which red blood drips gently downwards, but in her right hand she is holding a long sharp icicle of spun sugar which she is sucking greedily. From my apron pocket I take a kerchief, and gently enfold her left hand. I wipe away both the glass and the blood, which later I will sew into the quilt for the next woman. I bind up her wounds. There is a long pause.

'I can give you a spell against morning sickness,' I say.

'Thank you,' she replies. 'I would appreciate that.'

There is another long pause, and then she says, 'Thank you. Goodbye.'

I say, 'You'll be back.'

She considers this then asks, 'Whatever for?'

'How should I know yet, but you will be back. Again and again, for ever.'

She looks at the splinter of sugar in her hand and sucks it voluptuously. Then she turns, crosses the clearing and goes back into the forest. I think I have seen the last of her and stand recovering my energy from the gentle warmth of the sun, but after a few moments she reappears from behind a tree; she waves her sugar-candy shard at me and calls out, quite gently, 'Goodbye for now then, Angel Maker.' And she goes away leaving me cackling in my clearing, with yet another window to cook. And another long wait.

Well, it has been a long story. I don't know even now if it has made clear the most important thing. I love her so much, now and always.

THE EIGHTH PLANET

❡

We see the eighth planet as Colombus saw America from the shores of Spain. Its movements have been felt, trembling along the far reaching line of our analysis, with a certainty hardly inferior to that of ocular demonstration.
John Herschel, President of the British Association, son of William Herschel, musician and astronomer.
10 September 1846

In the end he said, quite calmly, at breakfast one morning, that he thought he would go back to London later that afternoon: he did not mean for a trip or even a visit, he meant for good, he meant goodbye and possibly even, Thank you for having me.

I said nothing; I just looked at him and realised with some deep and abiding sadness that my main emotion was of relief. He finished his coffee and went upstairs to start packing. I put on my wellington boots – black, I would like to say, not green – and walked down to the shop to get the newspaper, and, ah God, it was a lovely, lovely morning. It was bright and clean as some days in late March can be, the sky pale blue and the branches of the hedgerow trees apparently getting fatter, pregnant with buds that are not yet even palest green, and the larch wood across the hillside was pink with promise and, despite my best efforts to tell myself that he was a bastard and my great love affair had come to a nasty end and everything was tragic, all I felt was a heart-lifting joy in the sparkly dew drops and a sweet pleasure at the thought of being alone again.

Even now I don't really understand why it turned out so horrendous. We went in with such high hopes, the hopes, we

11

thought, of maturity and good sense, no adolescent romantics we; two people with meshing needs and a deep sense of sexual attraction. And for the first couple of months it was wonderful; we even reached the point of talking about selling both our houses and finding somewhere that would be ours. Once in the middle of a snowy night just before Christmas when we had been out, muffled up like children, we had even mentioned the possibility of having a baby – or rather, to be precise, he had said, 'Let's build a snowman. I need to get in practice for when we have a child.' We had started to roll one of those progressive balls that get larger and larger and leave neat black lines weaving about the lawn, but in the end we had gone to bed instead.

And then quite unexpectedly we had gone into a place of hell; of meanness and hatefulness. Never, never have I felt for anyone the hatred, the irresistible hatred, that I felt for him and he for me: a hatred that could not permit a decent withdrawal, that could not even confine itself to scathing, hurtful arguments but erupted into appalling violence that was mutual and savage and unlovely. But was also completely engaging, an eyeball-to-eyeball clash of the whole of two people, locked together like the lovers in Dante's *Inferno*. I, I who had always loathed romanticism, that 'all for love and the world well lost' stuff, I who preferred relationships to be domestic and comfortable and not distracting, who liked my sex civilised and preferred to do the crossword puzzle anyway. So, on top of everything else, there was this deep shame in both of us, and more simply embarrassment that we should see ourselves and each other like this. And for me at least, a complete loss of identity; quite literally I did not know who I was and I had done no work all winter and could not imagine how I thought I was going to pay for that.

And after some months of that it suddenly went away. There was a great calm after the storm and we looked at each other more in amazement than in anything else; a sort of terrified surprise, a kind of Who *is* this, who can have reduced me to such depths? And we were courteous and civil with each other and there was simply nothing there. We even made love with a tenderness and concern for the other's pleasure, and had long and sincere conversations about where and what each of us might do next, and he fixed new shelves for my kitchen and I knitted him a huge Aran sweater, with elaborate and elegant cables up back and front. And now, when we had so to speak completed our rest cure, it was time for him to go back to London.

I walked back from the village shop with the newspaper under my arm and a couple of packets of cigarettes in my pocket and recognised that I was making new plans, plans for work and plans for the vegetable garden, even plans for a summer holiday. And that felt so good. I put the newspaper on the kitchen table and called up the stairs to him, and then I went into the garden to pick him some daffodils to take back to his cold flat in London, just as I would have done for any week-end guest. And indeed I started thinking about week-end guests and friends that I had not seen for months, and I could feel something in my lower neck relax, and my feet spread themselves out inside my spacious wellington boots. I went inside and dumped the flowers in a bucket in the back kitchen, took off my boots and padded in my socks to my pinboard to find the train timetable.

While I was standing there he came downstairs and I noticed with an abstract pleasure how beautiful he still was, conscious that I had not noticed this for weeks, even months. He had been one of the most beautiful undergraduates of our year when I had first known him twenty years ago. A wild glamour that had somehow never gone away, not even now he was cleaner and tidier and richer than any of us could ever have dreamed of. Whereas I, it would have to be said, had not aged so well, and indeed was sloppier, dirtier and cosier than I would have dared to be then, when even my uniform jeans had about them a circumspection and a willingness to be checked out and inspected by anyone who cared. We had been in one of those Trotskyite groupings, those joyfully puritanical, fragmenting, shifting, passionate student groups in the late sixties; not the guitars and marijuana sorts, although actually we did lots of both of those, more the beer and theory until three in the morning, our radical paths crisscrossing for a while, an alliance forming between us, then a friendship. And anything was possible in those giddy optimistic times when the mornings had edges so sharp that you could cut yourself on the daylight. I had even

13

slept with him a couple of times, before other things intervened.

Later I had got married and divorced and I met him again last year at one of those dinner parties in London where people envy each other their success while feeling slightly guilty about their own; friendship networks so old and intimate that the difficulties and differences can collapse into wild mirth at an instant, or can flare into fights which, however vicious at the time, will not actually change anything nor prevent the same people coming together again pretty soon, at an identical but different pine kitchen table where everyone tries to keep secret to themselves that they wished the wine was a little better. Property prices and psychoanalysis are mentioned shyly as perhaps our parents mentioned sex, but once on the table so to speak it turns out that we are all enormously knowledgeable. And I do not wish to sound so mean, because they are my friends and indeed I am one of them and would not be otherwise. And we are all anti-Thatcherites and those that have them struggle desperately to keep their children within the state school system, and see the all-too-frequent failures of others to succeed as being somehow like a rather nasty disease – compassion and sorrow the appropriate response rather than that clear bell-like anger we could all touch so easily once upon a time.

It was actually quite odd that he and I had not met in this way at any time before. We had that night, I remember, a conversation about who had actually believed in 1969 that The Revolution was real and immediate, and half-sheepishly both of us admitted a complete and profound faith, and had smiled wryly at each other, though whether at our once naivety or our failure to live up to so fine and pure a commitment was not so totally obvious. But it had been, you must understand, a credo, a way of living, which had after all been sincere and which had also been expensive to abandon and left us fretful still. Later I drove him home, since Hackney is basically on the way to Ipswich, and since he does not own a car and it was late. And outside his charming Victorian terraced artisan's cottage (through lounge, 2 beds, kitchen/diner, bathroom, gas-fired central heating, tastefully refurbished preserving many period features. I know how mean and catty I am and to punish myself have to admit that my cottage has a thatched roof) we encountered one of those odd surges of pure desire that are entirely mutual and he said to me, 'We have unfinished business, you and I.' And whatever that had been, it was now at least well and truly finished.

So I could smile at his beauty and, indeed, at him, not without some considerable pleasure when he came down the stairs into my kitchen. He had the newspaper in his hand and an apologetic grin on his face.

He asked, 'What time is the late train?'

I inspected the timetable and told him. 'Why?' I asked.

'We could see Neptune tonight. With the telescope.' He flapped the paper gently.

He would not ask to stay another night. I would have resented it bitterly if he had. But he would very much like to see Neptune with the telescope. It was an odd thing about the telescope. It had belonged to the uncle of mine who had left me the cottage and had been waiting along with other treasures when I arrived. I had kept it only because it was a very beautiful object, with lovely brass bits and pieces: there is something extraordinarily lovely to me in Victorian scientific instruments, along with clocks and musical boxes, where the desire that something should work perfectly is not made a reason for not having it look wonderfully wrought. Properly speaking, it is probably, like the crinoline, merely an example of conspicuous consumption, a public way of saying, Look how much I can afford to spend, but in its presence I could never focus on that but only on the pleasure that looking at it gave me. I never used it for anything, indeed found it well-nigh impossible to see anything through it, even the larch trees across the hill, but he loved it functionally. At the golden beginning of our relationship when we had first come down to the cottage he had fallen on it with joy and arrived the next time with a small pile of star charts and books. Back in the autumn he had spent hours looking through it, while I had curled on the sofa enjoying the anticipation of lust, the mounting excitement of waiting. He would try to show me what he was looking at sometimes, but proximity and darkness were usually too much for us. I had not proved myself an adept at amateur astronomy.

'Is that special?' I asked him now.

'Special enough for the late train.' After a short pause he said, 'Please.'

'All right then,' I said, 'I can drive you to the station after that.'

Much later, when we had had tea and were waiting for the darkness, he said, 'I'll tell you something about Neptune that you may not like. It disproves the whole thing about learning coming from experience, theory being grounded on what actually is. They discovered it by pure theory.'

I asked him what he meant.

'In 1781 William Herschel became the first person in history to discover a planet, Uranus. He discovered it as you might expect, as most things are discovered, by well informed accident and good luck, by looking, just by looking at everything through his telescope, which he had made himself because he couldn't afford to buy one. He looked and looked and thought about what he saw and he discovered a planet – planets don't twinkle, you see, and under sufficient magnification they show a disk not a point of light. Well, after he had found it, other astronomers tried reasonably enough to plot its orbit, but wherever they thought it ought to be it wasn't. So they worked out in total abstract that it was being pulled out of its expected orbit by the gravity of another invisible planet, somewhere out there, somewhere beyond the known limits of the sun's cosmic system. Somewhere so far out that you could not see it with the naked eye. And in principle it should be possible to work out exactly where it was. So this young mathematician called John Couch Adams did just that in 1845. Sort of typical academe, he could not get anyone to look for it for him. Some Frenchman called Urbain Leverrier worked it out too. So they knew it was there; they knew it was there, and exactly where theoretically before they found it.'

I may not need to mention that he was a teacher of extraordinary verve and energy, whose lectures were well attended and whose books, given their academic abstraction, sold remarkably well. He loved to impart information like this.

And I, I loved being told stories like this. He had known that too when he had said I might not like it. That was a tease, because he knew I was a sucker when it came to this sort of incident. I pushed him for all the details he knew; I imagined poor John Adams trekking around the astronomers of Britain saying, 'There it is, there it is, look, look it's your job to look', and no one believing him enough to bother to get into their observatories and look for it. I find it odd how little people ever seem to want to detect things they're meant to detect. Like the Yorkshire Ripper, for example. How on the available evidence could they have failed to find Sutcliffe? You collect all the evidence and then you almost wilfully fail to act on it. Only amateurs, lovers, in their chambers on Baker Street, half sozzled with cocaine, actually want to solve mysteries. So I said, 'Tell me, tell me.'

And sitting by the fireplace in my little cottage with a big mug of tea between his hands and his lovely high-boned face turned away from me and towards the flames, he told me more things.

He told me that Neptune has two moons: one is tiny and called Miranda, and the other is huge and called Triton; and Triton is the only object in the cosmic universe that revolves in the opposite direction. Of all the planets and all their satellites, only Triton has the imagination to spin backwards. He told me that Neptune has not rings, like Saturn and Jupiter and Uranus but arcs, little bits of broken-up ring, material all that way away striving to turn itself from a strip into a clump – matter that desires to be a satellite. He told me that Neptune is a liquid planet, its surface entirely covered by water. He told me that at the bottom of this ocean, which functions as a blanket, it is so hot and so compressed that the methane at its core is perhaps breaking up into carbon atoms and hydrogen atoms and the carbon is being pressed into diamond crystals. Far away, beyond the furthest seeing of the naked eye, there is the jewel-encrusted underwater cavern that the ancients dreamed of for their sea god, Neptune.

And this they knew from pure theory alone. Even Voyager 2 has not yet travelled long enough or far enough to see Neptune in any detail.

And in the freezing night we turned off the lights and he looked through the telescope, referring at first to the newspaper and then to his huge space atlas. And suddenly he gave a tiny shiver of pleasure and I knew he had found it. He looked for a moment and then fixed the telescope, twiddling one of the elegant brass knobs effortlessly and without taking his eye away from the lens.

'Come and see,' he said, stretching out one arm and tucking me into the fold of his body, as I had so many times been tucked before. But his energy was flowing not towards me but towards the whole dense sky. I put my eye against the optic and at first I could see nothing, then I could see too much, a million too many stars, a great war in heaven, and I was almost terrified. And keeping his arm round me, warm and gentle, he told me very quietly what to look for, how to find Neptune and suddenly there it was: a tiny distant pale bluish disc floating out there. It did not twinkle or waver. I was amazed. Even if I never saw him again, he would have given me this gift, this sight of a new world known, discovered and created by theory.

'Thank you,' I said with real pleasure.

'No, thank you,' he said, and I turned within his arms and we exchanged a kiss so pure and tender that I have never known anything like it.

It was so perfect a moment that it became immediately imperative that he should catch the train. He pushed the lens cover over the telescope and took the stairs two at a time in his energetic determination to get his bags down and into the car. I helped him, not even bothering to say we had plenty of time. There was a sort of panic and unreasonableness about our haste which seemed appropriate to us both; but as soon as we were both in the car I realised that I had forgotten to give him the flowers I had picked that morning. I leapt out again and ran back into the empty cottage. When I saw the telescope still standing on its tripod at the window I knew I had to give it to him – not the flowers after all, but that. I folded it up and packed it into its leather box. He came to the door, impatient to be gone, and saw what I was doing. He didn't even question me, it was so right. He said thank you once again and then came over and squatting together on the floor we did up the leather straps and brass buckles with infinite and delicate care. Then together we carried it out to the car and laid it on the back seat. Then we both scrambled back into the car and belted off; I knew I was over-revving the engine, and that it was foolish to take the bend by the old mill stream at such a pace, but there was a desperate compulsion about it. I wanted him out of my life, right then and there. And I could feel him beside me wanting the same thing.

The silence in the car felt painfully oppressive. I heard myself jabbering suddenly, endless words pumping out. I said, 'Now I'll tell you a story, or at least a thought, about Neptune. If it was discovered in 1846 there is a wild appropriateness about that: just two years, enough time for it to sneak into public consciousness, before 1848; and Neptune was the god of revolutions, of storms, of raising new worlds out of the ocean deeps. Homer says that when Neptune issued from the sea and crossed the earth in three strides, the mountains and the forests trembled. He was the god who was always restless and invented the horse as a symbol of war and slaughter. So maybe there really is something in astrology.'

He laughed. I drove slower. The twistings of the country lane had, almost without our noticing it, imposed some sort of calmness on my driving. The desperate urgency evaporated, flowing off into the dark night around us.

I asked him, 'How did you get into stars, anyway? It does seem a rather improbable hobby for the bright young scientific socialist.'

'Oh well,' he replied, apparently laughing, 'scientific socialism got all buggered up. You bloody feminists did that, punched holes right through the middle of the fabric of the thing, didn't you? Where else is there for a scientific marxist to go but off to explore new worlds and the further away the better? Like the Levellers after the collapse of the Commonwealth. You take your mysticism to the country and bury it in the mud; I take my science to the skies and bury it in darkness.'

I glanced at him and his beautiful face was tense not just with anger but with pain.

I said, 'You may not believe this, but underneath it all, and I don't know how the hell to go about it and I don't live it on the flesh of experience as I said we ought to and I'm a fat cat and will greet the Revolution, if it comes, with tears for what I'm losing, rather than the more traditional dancing in the streets, but . . .

19

but I still do believe that the overthrow of capitalism is The Project.'

And he said, 'I know you do. The question is, do I?'

And after a little while longer I said, 'It is sad. I somehow cannot escape the feeling that we all, all of us, all our generation of people, deserved better than we got. And yet we got so much.'

'*Sic transit gloria mundi*,' he said a little peevishly.

'No,' I said, 'that's not what I mean.'

'No,' he said, 'I know it isn't, but I'm bloody well not going to say thank you again. More like the Transit of f—ing Venus or something.'

And that was enough of that. So we talked inconsequentially of this and that, friends and acquaintances, gossip and memories. Suddenly he started to tell me about Neptune again. I thought I didn't really want to hear that, but it was better than nothing and we were still a considerable distance from the train station. I half listened as he talked about densities, and gravities, and mass versus size. And suddenly I heard something in his voice, a sharpening, a precision, perhaps even a kind of nervousness, and I knew he was telling me something that was infinitely precious to him. He was telling me about Neptune's vast moon, Triton, whom from his previous description I had assumed to be something of the joker in the pack, eternally revolving backwards against all possible odds. And yes, yes, that was part of it, obviously; but also infinitely no. There's some astronomer in Haiti who spent a great deal of time speculating – both looking at and guessing about – on Triton. Now he said to me, in the apparently enclosed world of the car rushing through the countryside, he said, 'It is a world of chilly oceans, whole oceans of liquid nitrogen. Away out there, those icy oceans coloured red, vivid crimson, by organic matter that we do not yet understand, rocked with tides beyond our moon space, infinitely pulled by a different, extenuated, frail force of gravity, and riding majestic those great rollers, silent because there is no breaking shore, there is no hearer for their thunder, riding the crimson oceans are the stately blue white icebergs of another place.'

He said all that and I, to my own surprise, said, 'Frozen methane.'

20

You probably understand by now that we had been trying all these months to be together – it had been an investment of great importance to us both, had taken us both into a new place of self-knowing – and now, too late to be of any use, in that extraordinary and almost casual reversal – my science, his poetry – we almost succeeded. If I had been able, just then, to take both hands off the steering wheel and show him how I had, once, a world away, oh hell, a cosmos away almost, in a small ship, seen the dignified and blue-white icebergs of our own planet, bobbing too gigantic for the word itself, seen them break themselves with a deep gonging sound off the master ice, the glacier ice, and swan, white as their own chosen style, down the great green – oh *so* green – drift waters of the Arctic Ocean, I think we might even have gone home and tried again. You know, that is the magic of incongruence, where two pieces of the apparently seamless garment of social reality do not quite fit together, and through the unknown gap comes seeping – well, what can I call it? the unexpected, the redemptive, the bizarre but also the welcome – oh well, comes seeping Joy. Like lava from between the dense, heavy, immeasurably shifting and dishonest plates of the earth's surface. But you know how it is really too – I was driving; I had responsibilities; there was a sharp bend, concentration-requiring; and then it was too late, or not appropriate, or something. That's the way it goes, all randomly and inexplicably.

As it was we were both delighted. And we damn nearly missed that train.

SEAL-SELF

❦

*In Cleveland it was well known that any wild goose which
flew over Whitby would instantly drop dead; and that to
catch a seal it was first necessary to dress as a woman.*
Keith Thomas, *Man and the Natural World*

It is cold when he wakes, stirred from forgotten dreams by the
deep whirring in the air. The goose flocks are driving north
again. It is cold and still dark, too dark to see the great wide
arrowheads, spread wide, not yet regathered since they had split
up to avoid Whitby, but he can hear them and he shivers. They
stir his blood each equinox with their coming and going, up
there, out there, beyond. He does not know where and he could
not imagine. Last week he had seen the falling stars, the serene
and magic performance of the heavens to celebrate the turning of
the year. And after the falling stars the wild geese, uncountable
also, will pass over along the pale coastline. For the next week
they will appear, from the south, at dawn and at dusk, through
the night watches and in the morning, as swift as falling stars
flighting northwards towards the cold wind. And after the wild
geese have passed the seal mothers will surge up from the icy
water and lay their pups on the great flat sands below. And
he . . . but he does not want to think about it.

He twisted into himself seeking what warmth there still might
be in the bed, wrapping his arms around himself, deliberately
seeking the safety of sleep, but the deep whirring noise over the
cottage roof continued unabated until it was fully dawn.

His world is shaped by the stripes. Green stripe. Yellow-gold

23

stripe. Lead-coloured stripe. Blue stripe. Across the stripes, at right-angles to them, ran another stripe, invisible but every bit as tangible; the fierce east wind that rushed in from far away across the ocean, coming at him, vicious and greedy, coming in a straight and evil line, down the sky, the sea, the sand, the fields. May God have mercy on his soul. He crosses himself, half scared, half scornful, for this is old women's thinking, and he is ashamed; and men now do not cross themselves, for times have changed, and his mouth curls in scorn of his mother and her fussing ways, for he is a man, and when the goose flocks are passed over and the seals come to play on the beaches, he will prove he is a man.

For the next ten days the wild geese pass over. He knows they are watching him, his friends, the geese, even the rising sun. His mother. In the village when he passes across the square the young women look at him, curious and questioning. The tawny maiden from the high farmstead eyes him, direct and challenging. She is taller than he is, and her legs run up under her skirt, legs so slender and long that they must lead somewhere good. She tosses her head in the pale April sunshine and diamonds scatter from her hair. He is bewitched by her long cool stare. As he carries the milk pail she passes by, almost brushing against him, and her clear voice bells sweetly to her friend, 'They say the first of the seal mothers are come to the sand dunes. I would love a sealskin cloak this year.' He hates her suddenly and brilliantly, bright as the April sunshine, but his penis stirs and he watches her breasts. She smiles at him, promising him. And if not her then another. They all promise him together.

Last year he could not bring himself to do it. It is not the killing; he has cut pigs' throats, catapulted birds out of the sky, snared hares, wrung chicken necks, drowned kittens, baited bears, put his evil-snouted ferret to the rabbits' warrens. It is the other. They do not understand. His mother had smiled last year when he had tried to tell her. She had laid out the apparel for him even. His stomach feels sick to think about it. His dreams fill with it. And it must be this spring, for by next year his beard will be upon him. Now is the time. He knows it. He is frightened. For it is well known that to catch a seal it is first necessary to dress as a woman.

24

He wakes again in the darkness as before, and there is silence; the whirring of the goose flocks has vanished northwards, and though it is still cold there is a new softness in the air. His fear is very present to him. He strips off his clothes and stands naked. He pulls on his mother's skirt and arranges it at his waist, it falls lumpenly, ugly, and his hairy feet appearing at the bottom strike him as ungainly and ludicrous. He knows, blindingly as dawn, what his fear is. It is pleasure. It is pleasure and desire. He tiptoes to his mother's kist, and takes for himself her boned corsets, her linen hose, her full Sunday petticoats, her best bonnet.

Before he is half-dressed his hands are wet with his own juices: his fingers tangled with bodice ribbons and semen, his mind with delight and shame. But after that he knows that it must be done well and fully. He takes great care, padding his hips with fleece, tightening the corset with gentle concern. The skirt hangs better so. He chooses for himself breasts not too large, too heavy, but high and delicate like the tawny maiden from the high farm. He smiles for himself that smile of veiled promise that she gave him in the village square. Then when everything is ready he realises that it will not do. He takes off the petticoats and skirt again; he takes a hair-ribbon, soft satin smooth, the same rich rose colour as the chaffinch's breast, that his mother brought home from the Whitby Fairings; she never wore it, it was too fine for her, she said, she wanted it only because it was a pretty thing and no one bought her pretty things any more. He ties it now gently round his penis, which is soft and pleased and sleepy, and draws it back between his legs, folding his testicles carefully. He feels the flat firm skin behind them and knows that there should be a hole, a place of darkness and wet that he will never know. It cannot be helped. He attaches the other end of the ribbon firmly to the bottom hole in the back of the corset. Now when he pulls on yet again the skirt and petticoat he knows that it is almost right. Shoes he must do without, for he will not mar his own loveliness with cloggy boots but none of his mother's will fit him. But stockinged feet are charming for a maid out in the fields at daydawn.

As he passes the parlour he sees in the half light himself in the mirror glass, gold curls fluffing out under the sweet bonnet with

25

its delicately ruched and pleated inner brim. How pretty she is, he thinks, so much prettier than the tawny maid from the high farmstead. He smiles. How pretty I am, she thinks, and she raises the latch craftily and skips out, silent and dainty, into the waiting springtime.

The preparation has taken longer than was planned. Now it is dawn already; the great stripes of the countryside have already divided themselves, though not yet into colours, only into different greys. But there is a ribbon, laid tidily between the grey stripe of sea and the paler grey stripe of sky, a rose pink ribbon holding the world in shape, the day spring whence the sun will be born.

She shivers in the cold dawn and wishes that she had a sealskin cloak to snuggle in, a cloak made from the softness of baby seal, white and thick and dappled. A sealskin cloak trimmed and fastened with rose pink ribbons, she thinks, and then she laughs at herself for her vanity. Nor would she wear one if he gave it to her, for seals are friends to honest women, and she is going now to meet her friend Seal Woman and greet the new Seal Child who will have been carried in the deep waters all through the winter, wrapped in thick sweet blubber and rocked in a secret bay between the promontories of her mother's pubic bones, safe within the greater ocean. And who would now be pupped in the soft golden sand, clumsy and enchanting, pug-faced, soft-furred, playful and unafraid. No woman of sense or worth would accept a sealskin cloak, not from the King himself were he to come to the cold coastland north of Whitby and hear the wind rush in from far across the ocean; nor would she wear one and mock the mourning of Seal Woman for her child.

So she laughs, though kindly, at herself and her vanity and walks across the grey meadows towards the seaside; and as she walks the light seeps gently into the air and the grass turns towards green and the birds begin to sing and the sea sedge and saxifrage are pale pinky mauve and the celandines are yellow. The pink ribbon beyond the sea widens and pales and the broad sweep of the sky overhead is almost as white and pure as the frothed edges of her petticoats, bleached out with love and joy.

Closer to, the line, which from the cottage seems so precisely drawn between grass and sea, is blurred, indefinite, hesitant. First there is grass and woolly sheep still huddled against the night, then there are scrubby plants mixed in with bare patches of earth, of sand, then there is mostly sand with the occasional bold push or outcrop of reedy grass, and then almost unnoticeably there is only sand, great reaches of it in rolling hills, swirled into fantastic shapes by the long-drawn wind from the sunrise side of the ocean. And finally the hillocks settle, flattened out by the waves, and there is a wide wet beach changing constantly with the long pushes and tugs of the tide.

And when she comes at last to the very end of the dunes, to the edge of the tide beach, she heaves a great sigh of relief, coming home, united in her belly with the pushes and pulls of the tide, of the moon, of the great spaces of the sea. Quietly and easily she folds her legs, her skirt ballooning softly around her and sits in silence watching the long waves roll in, smooth and strong from out there, out beyond her eye view, and each wave is different and each wave is exactly the same for ever and ever and she feels calmed, rocked, soothed, contented.

And as she sits there, waiting for the sun to rise, the seals begin to emerge. Some from the sea where they had gone at her approaching, and some from the dunes where they had slept. Now they flop, heavy and clumsy, on the shining golden sand by the waterline. Some are still gravid, ponderous and careful, and some have already pupped and their tiny young lurch around them or frolic idiotically in the wave edges. Not thirty yards from the shore a mother seal floats on her back, her tail flapping balance against the wave tossings, her little white pup held, flipper-fast, against her breast to suckle. So water-graceful, land-clumsy; so strong, so tender; so like and so unlike herself. She forgot the reason and the manner of her coming and waited only on the movement of the tide and the rising of the sun.

'Good morning, my dear,' says Seal Woman, 'and welcome.'

She springs to her feet to curtsy.

'Hello,' says Seal Child. 'I'm new.'

And new she certainly is, but already with bright black eyes that look and see, and with flourished whiskers, moustaching out from her black nose, and dappled white-grey fur fluffed in the

27

sun. Barely two foot long, neatly constructed for an environment that cannot sustain her, at home in no element, timeless, lovable, perfect and preposterous. She smiles and reaches out a hand to touch Seal Child's nose.

And now, now he is meant now to take a stone and smash it down on Seal Child's head, blanking out the shiny eyes forever and carrying off the soft skin to the tawny maiden from the high homestead to wear as her victor's spoils, and to prove to the village that he has become a man, but she has forgotten this, lost in the wide free space of air and ocean, lost in the wide loving gaze of Seal Woman.

There is no need to talk much, or to talk of anything in particular. She sits, Seal Woman sprawls, and Seal Child suckles unhindered, occasionally wriggling or squeaking in delight. And all across the wet beach there are a hundred other seal mothers suckling, snoozing, sprawling, and now the gulls come swooping, wailing, to join them, and out on the breakers the older pups play and beyond that the sea pours in, in, in, a long solemn, musical procession, ancient and careful. And, quite suddenly, the sun rises.

Seal Child waggles her flippers in delight, tosses her tail, gambols a little. Seal Child says, 'Will you play with me?'

'Yes,' she says, 'yes, please.'

'Mother, come too,' begs Seal Child.

'Of course,' says Seal Woman.

So together the three of them go down to the seashore and plunge in. And suddenly she is not woman to woman with Seal Woman, but child to child with Seal Child. In the water it is a new Seal Child, graceful, strong, rhythmic; suddenly no longer little and sweet but powerful, fast, the fur no longer soft and fluffy but streamlined, completed. Together she and Seal Child splash and paddle in the breaking water, dance in and out of the foam, going deeper, deeper, deeper in. The waves mount around her, lifting her skirts gently up and down, until they are soaked through and dragging at her legs; her balance fails and she falls into the next wave, is lifted by it, raised up, brought down, and left as it runs on in towards the sparkling sands. When she realises that her feet will not touch the bottom again she is, for a

28

moment, scared and then it does not matter because she too can swim like a seal, strong and shapely, powerful in the water as never on the land. And deep new places opening in her lungs so that she can go down and under and be there unafraid.

And now they swim and swim; the dark cold waters are the breeding grounds of fishes who move in vast shoals hard to see. But flipping over and rising upwards the surface is a great starry sky, brighter and fiercer than the terrestrial constellations; where the water meets the air there is a barrier, a great spangled ceiling, chandeliered with light, with air, water, sun-fire sparkled. And turning downwards, down, down into the dark there is the everlasting silence, the great underwater drifts and waves and forces of currents unlit by the sunshine, and great still mountains, cliffs, ranges, beflowered in dark growths whose shadows deepen the green darkness and whose rhythms are from before the beginning of air breathing, and Seal Woman flows between her two children, guarding them, hovering over them, around them, protecting them, remembering them in the forgotten places. And there is no weight, no gravity, no memory, and deep, deep below there is the ocean floor whence they all came and whither they do not choose to go and they are carried above it joyfully, on the strength of their own limbs, wings, fins. And Seal Child, using flippers and nose, pulls away the ties on the sweet little bonnet and it floats a moment in the water, like a dark jelly fish, and is gone.

Then, on another shared thought, they all turn and shoot upwards, breaking the surface into sprinkled jewels, whooshing into sunlight, their lungs pulling in new fresh air, bobbing upon the surface and laughing together. And Seal Child, using tail and teeth, strips off the knitted hose and chases them playfully across the wave tops till they drift away.

They swim far north to the gathering and gossiping grounds of the salmon, under the shelter of the great ice pack, where the waters teem with microscopic life, and are greener than the grass. They swim among the mating places of the wild geese and see the cold slopes where the white swans winter. They watch the dignified icebergs sail regally out towards their death, glittering bravely in the bright sunlight, and they dine without effort on the

29

herring shoals that drift on unseen currents across the sub-polar waters. And Seal Child, using nose and mouth, nuzzles off the skirt and petticoats, the bodice and sleeves, and lazily they float away to provide refuge for some weary tern in some other distant sea.

And then they turn and drift slowly southwards, following the cold current that finds its way along the eastern coast of Scotland, leisurely riding the water and watching the ships in the distance break the tidy line of the horizon. And the sun comforts those bits of them that break the surface of the cold sea, so they turn on their backs and let their tummies feel the gentle spring warmth in the morning light. And they play in the rocky pools off Lindisfarne, the Holy Island; and watch the great gannets drop sixty vertical feet through the air, white streaks of power; and they tease the gaudy puffins who bob and wimble under those serene cliffs. And Seal Child, using tail and flippers and mouth and nose, unties the corset cords and pulls the garment off and with a weary sigh it sinks down and down to amuse poor drowned sailors from years and years ago.

And as they come back to their own golden beach to the north of Whitby, the end of the rose-pink ribbon, which she had tied to the corset and which had worked its way in between her buttocks, floats loose and drifts like the colourful seaweed in a coral lagoon two thousand miles away to the south and west. Seal Child plays with it as it dangles and they all laugh, riding in on the breakers and coming to rest at last on the sunny wet sand in the first early hours of the day. And Seal Woman and she lounge on the beach and talk of those things that women talk of when they have had good physical exercise and are met in magic places, while Sea Child frolics around them playing with the ends of the pink ribbon and with her penis.

Seal Child says, 'I love you.'

She says, 'I love you too.' All three of them grin peacefully. And it is simply true.

Seal Child is still very young. Love means warmth and cuddling and feeding. Seal Child scrambles up on to her body and tries to suckle from her, not finding flat breasts, small nipples or a soft furred chest anything out of the usual. She holds Seal

Child under the front flippers to steady her, feeling with great pleasure the softness of wet fur against her own belly. Seal Child's whiskers and soft mouth tickle, she giggles and rolls over with her; mother child; child puppy; child child; happy. Seal Child tries again to suckle, her mouth is round and pink, her lips firm and sweet against the nipple. And suddenly the soft and floppy penis, still bedecked with rose pink ribbon, springs up, awakened. She rolls over on to Seal Child who wriggles in the sand. Suddenly he looks up. Seal Woman is looking at him, not just with anger, but with great sadness and greater amazement. He springs to his feet, the ribbon still dangling.

'I'm sorry,' he says to Seal Woman.

'Come and play some more,' says Seal Child.

'No,' says Seal Mother.

Seal Child looks puzzled. She is about to start whining. She flops to her mother and finds there the milky sweetness she had been seeking; with enthusiasm she begins to feed.

'I'm sorry,' he says again.

'I have never been fooled before,' says Seal Woman. 'Why is it?'

'I was naked,' he says, beginning to be annoyed. 'You could have seen. You must have known.'

'That's not what counts,' says Seal Woman.

They are still. They both look out at the sea, where the waves break still. They both look at Seal Child sucking. For a last moment they both share equally the desire to protect the baby at all costs.

Feeling their attention on her, Seal Child breaks her sucking and grins. She flops affectionately over to him and for a moment Seal Woman just watches them. Seal Child tugs at the wet pink ribbon. His penis swells again.

'You must go now,' says Seal Woman sadly.

Seal Child, silky wet, rubs her flat face across his belly.

'I could cut it off,' he offers; and for a sweet moment of fear, excitement, desire, loss, he means it. Seal Child's snout snuffles downwards, nibble-mumbling his soft hair; her whiskers tickle him. His penis stirs, Seal Child and he giggle.

'No, that's not what counts,' says Seal Woman.

31

'No,' says Seal Child.

'No,' he agrees.

'Please,' he says.

Now, he thinks, now I should take up this heavy stone, that is here, by good fortune, here just beside me, here at hand, and bash in her head and strip out her blubber guts and carry home her soft sweet fur and have her forever and be a man. This is what I came for, he thinks, and his penis stirs again.

'Please,' he says, 'please let me stay.'

And if they will just do what he says, wants, needs, he thinks he will not have to hurt them.

'No,' says Seal Woman. She knows his thoughts but she is not afraid. She is angry-sad, sad-angry. 'No.'

They vanish.

They have taken from him even a moment of choice. The stone is there, round, heavy, fitted to his hand, but he had not decided. Round the very base of his penis, tangled in his golden pubic hair, is one long whisker caught underneath the rose pink ribbon, but he had not decided. He will never know what he would have decided.

It is full morning, suddenly, bright beyond bearing. On the golden stripe of the beach there is nothing but his golden body. Out in the leaden-coloured stripe he sees their leaden-coloured heads bob, spaniel-eyed, sad and smiling.

He goes home. He crosses out of the golden stripe and into the green one. No one sees his solemn, naked procession.

Later he says, 'It is well known that any wild goose which flies over Whitby will instantly drop dead; and that to catch a seal it is first necessary to dress as a woman.'

Later he says, 'I caught a seal, but then I let her go.' He does not know if they believe him; he does not know if he is a man.

HEART THROB

❋

Darkness.

A drum roll, distant, muffled within that darkness.

Then half bars of strange music, unformed lost notes, discordant, chaotic, but gentle, solemn, sweet: music from before the dawn of order, pre-creation music. A steady soft drum beat, the pulsing heart of life; but so quiet, so soft that the brain itself must be quieted to hear it. Three beautiful clear notes of a triangle and the darkness begins to shift as coloured smoke wafts dreamily. The high flat mountain comes into focus as pale and far away as the dawn and at the foot of the mountain Kalubini sits, the jewels of his turban catching the refractions of light within the swirling smoke. His face is still, timeless, serious. His knees are flat on the ground while his thighs support his feet in the eternal lotus posture; his palms on his knees are turned outwards and his thumb and index finger form a soft circle within which all the powers of the gods are held.

When there is enough light he begins to move, to gyrate smoothly in strange godlike movements, beyond the power of earth-bound, material bodies. He is snake in its litheness; he is pool of water in its rippled calm; he is frog in its alert stillness; he is palm tree in its mighty growth; he is power of mind and matter brought together. These are no vulgar contortions, they are the thoughts of a god awakening at dawn in the mystical east and bringing first himself and then the world to light and life.

The music becomes more orderly, fitting itself around the deep heart beat that holds all things together: Kalubini is the heart of the universe. His gentle remote expression never changes as he rises to his feet and moves forwards. He looks around, mildly curious, and then smiles. With his smile the light increases. He picks up a small earthenware bowl, plain reddish clay shaped into the inevitable full curve. He holds it between his two long hands, turning it this way and that, peering into its empty roundness. He smiles still, and then murmurs to the bowl. A white dove suddenly, almost shockingly, flies out of it. His expression does not change. He murmurs again. Another dove, very white in the still drifting coloured smoke. The pace of the music quickens almost imperceptibly, and suddenly there are more and more doves, they flow like a waterfall out of the small round bowl; they rest on Kalubini's turban, on his silken cloak; they peck on the ground. Then all at once in a moment of pure flight they take off together, circle and alight in a small flowering tree which becomes a living rustle of movement, bird and flower together, serene and vital.

Kalubini seems hardly to notice. He fixes his solemn attention on the bowl again and from it now flows, flashing gold and green, a shoal of tiny fish, which he pours gently but steadily into an ornate glass tank near his left hand. When the tank is apparently fuller than it can hold with dancing fish he looks down at his bowl again. For the first time his face assumes an identifiable expression – a wry and amused disappointment. He tosses the bowl aside carelessly and shards of clay tinkle on the ground. He finds another, larger bowl and appears contented with it. Again he turns it slowly in his arms, examining its smooth glazed surface inside and out with apparent disinterest. But when he murmurs to it a cat, pure white and sleek, erupts from the empty space, alights briefly on his shoulder and vanishes. A black dog follows, slim and delicate as a greyhound, tiny as a terrier. It jumps down and curls contentedly at his feet. Kalubini does not smile now but looks infinitely sad. He puts the bowl down on the ground. He whips off his silk cloak and crumples it into the bowl, folding it down until the bowl seems full with it, and then he turns away. Suddenly the heart throb of the drum beat stirs, the

34

silk ripples as though touched by a breeze and begins to rise. From the curved interior of the bowl which did not seem large enough to hold even the little dog a woman emerges, stunningly lovely. Kalubini turns back again and his face is wreathed in delight. He beckons to her and she steps out of the bowl towards him. He raises his right hand imperiously and she starts to dance, her veils parting just enough to show the glittering jewel in her navel and the bright scarlet caste mark on her forehead. Her legs are long and bare, her torso breathtaking, her feet elegant beyond dreaming, her face with its long sloped eyes and perfect mouth is fixed on him and she dances a slow swaying dance of the eternal feminine from the ancient civilisations far over the seas.

The music quickens now and her dance becomes wilder and wilder. She turns from him, dancing away, her eyes fixed on the outside world, on the morning and the space of the universe. It becomes almost a coquettish dance as she realises that there is a whole world to enchant and not just him. Kalubini is furious, he reaches for her but she slips away. He cannot bear it – she has insulted and rejected a god. He leaps upon her, tossing her into the air as though her weight were nothing and his strength infinite. She arches upwards and falls back into his arms, where she lies laughing at him. His anger is the fountain of the world; the calm has vanished from his face and has become replaced by a terror, an awfulness. She realises this and becomes frightened, but he remains stern. He throws her down on a small platform worked with mysterious kabbalistic designs. He covers her again with his cloak and then slams over her a great lacquered lid which he wields as though it were made of straw.

The music stops abruptly. But still he is not content. His fury is manifest in his agitated pacing, in his grinding teeth and in his flashing eyes. With a shocking suddenness he whips out a huge curved sword. He brandishes it wildly, and it slices through the leaves of the tree, fluttering the roosting birds; it slices through the sleeve of his own flowing garment and the shorn silk droops sadly to the ground. After a moment's hesitation he slashes at the lacquered lid and the sword carves through it; then he is hacking, stabbing, chopping in his wrath. From inside comes one painful moan, and a small bleeding hand drops over the edge of the platform. He hurls bits of the lid, bits of his own silk cloak, bits of her veiling across the ground. He is gleeful now and triumphant. He leaps and dances, prances and cavorts in his victory over her.

Abruptly he ceases. He hears a few bars of the music which she had danced to. Suddenly the tiny dog, who has lain peacefully throughout the devastation, lifts up its head and howls. Kalubini is struck; he bends to stroke the dog tenderly and when he raises his head he is weeping. Crystal tears pour from his eyes, but as they fall they turn into jewels, diamonds and pearls, which he gathers in his hands and throws away disgusted. Slowly, sadly, he starts to collect the pieces of his love from where they have fallen. He picks up the little hand and kisses it sorrowfully. He places all the fragments in his bowl. The music starts again. The little dog trots over to the bowl and sits beside it, his head cocked hopefully. Kalubini stands by the bowl murmuring quietly and gently. The coloured smoke begins to move again, the music to settle down, the throbbing of the drum to find its previous rhythm. There is a blinding flash of lightning, a great drum roll of thunder, and there she is! Whole and beautiful as ever. She casts herself into his arms with ecstatic delight. He catches her to his breast and rains godlike kisses upon her. The music reaches a crescendo of excitement; the drum throb, strong and clear now, celebrates the power of life and love. Leaping with joy, tossing her high with easy virility, he carries her away; his face is like a little boy's who got what he wanted for his birthday after all. Vibrant with delight, with no eyes for anything except each other, the couple disappear and only the drum beat continues for another few moments

It is a terrific act though I say so myself. He's a very skilled illusionist and between us we've managed to pack in almost everything a modern variety audience wants – oriental mysticism, suspense, a coherent scenario, some effective stunts, a touch of pathos and a bit of implied nooky without passing the boundaries. Managements like it because it doesn't need a cast of thousands and almost every damn theatre in the world can scrape up a mountain scene drop – with our lighting we can pretty much get away with an alpine set if we have to. And, well, I'll tell you what it is, the act has a certain something that really goes over: 'most romantic act in town', some newspaper called it the other day . . . It's what's between the two of us really; whenever we go on, it's there, like a third person in the act, our relationship with each other, and that comes over, a kind of romantic excitement. Neither of us had it before; well, I know I didn't, and I don't think he can have, because as far as the tricks go he hasn't learned anything from me; he is very good; but he never really made it big. We met two years ago on the West Coast: I was doing a spot of 'exotic dancing' – well, to be frank I was a call-girl in a honky-tonk with a little speciality number. He was working what was basically a parlour act: neat tricks, pretty – especially with the pigeons and the goldfish, a suave evening-dress conjurer with pretensions to class. Not bad. Funny we ever got together really; we met fooling around at somebody's place one night, and it just came to us both, the whole thing. We put the act together on the road coming east. It went pretty well in Chicago, though it wasn't all fixed then and we were still having trouble with the music – before we thought of the drum heart beat to hold it all together. But by Philadelphia we knew we were on to something big and managements started knowing it too, and we were getting good billings and agents after us and that stuff and New York was just wonderful. We played Keith's six months straight and we were hot.

Then with the war ending and that let's-go-to-Europe fever everywhere, and we were both pretty pleased with ourselves and thought, 'Why not? Let's give it a go.' Berlin, Amsterdam, Paris, London. Two months we've been playing the Oxford and we don't see much sign of it coming off yet. So you could say, I would say, that things were pretty good. In fact there are only two flies in the ointment. One of them is him and the other is me.

The snag with him is that he's beginning to believe it all: I think it was that yoga thing we put in for the opening, and that crazed teacher he went to, who gave him all this bit about mystical meditation and oneness with the universe and the power of the will in harmony with matter and that stuff. I mean, it is quite impressive when he puts his ankles over his neck or folds his rib cage into accordian pleats, but it's not the key to the universe, frankly. It doesn't make him a god; it doesn't even make him a real oriental Indian, for heaven's sake. I mean, the fact that he believes it may help the act, but he can't lay it down when we come off. I should have put my foot down when he first started wearing that damn turban off stage, in public, on the ship coming over, but he told me 'publicity' and 'image' and things, and it was like music to my ears, quite honestly. And where did it leave me? I mean, here I was, for the first time in my life, able to afford a few decent things, and we were in Europe, really classy things I mean, but no, because if he's going to be an Indian then of course I have to be one too, don't I? And Indian women don't go out in public, and Indian women wear saris and veils and keep their mouths shut and just adore their men. And if I argue with him he goes blank on me, his eyes narrow up and his face goes cold and I . . .

Well, I told you there was a snag about me too, and the damn stupid thing is that I've fallen for him. I mean really, the big thing. It's too pathetic, actually: I'm thirty-two years old and I've been around and I wasn't brought up sentimental either. My ma was a tough lady and she always warned me against love and told me straight out what it could do to a woman. And here I am, I'm like a little kid about him. Well, no, not exactly like a little kid, but . . . I don't know how to put it, quite: I never had much schooling and I don't read all the stuff that he reads or know all those lovely words, but he makes me feel. Just that, not good or bad, not happy or sad, but he does make me feel. So much that the feeling is for itself, it doesn't seem to matter what it is. So when his face goes cold or he turns away from me and won't listen or look or touch, then something in me dies. And when he comes back then I'm so happy and grateful that I do anything he wants, anything, anything.

So what with him thinking he's a god, and me thinking he's a god, it's not surprising that three-quarters of the punters end up thinking he's a god too; but for them, of course, it's also just a turn – a classy twenty minutes in the middle of a good variety show and them all snuggled down in the lovely plush seats and afterwards they can just go home.

Well, we go home too, of course, but it doesn't always end

38

there. Of course we were lovers right from the start. Why pay for two beds when you need only pay for one? I said, all bright and brassy, the first week we were on the road. To be honest, he wasn't much into it then, I was the one who knew what we were doing, or meant to be doing, just like I was the one pushing the act, shaping it up, you know, because although he's skilful at his own trade he doesn't – or he didn't, anyway – have that feel for a good act that I do. I mean, even when I was just one more little exotic dancer selling something else, I knew, I knew how to put it over. It was when we got the sword trick going, when he got to slash me into little bits twice a night, six nights a week, that things changed. He loved it, he really loved it. And he was wonderful – you could see what it did to him. He took on a new something, a new power with it. And he brought that home to us. He started to change, to take more – to take the lead more, I suppose. And it was wonderful at first. His hands so clever and his body so flexible and I melted for him, I couldn't get enough. He was strong and fit and suddenly he knew exactly what he was doing, and if some of that went a little further than I had expected, well, I found that quite exciting too. He was focused on me, only me: only I could meet that need in him. We have to be a bit careful, of course, because the costume doesn't cover all that much; but there are things and places, he sucks my blood like a vampire and he needs me to feed him; as he eats me I am eaten by him, I become part of him and . . . Well, of course he would stop if I asked him to, I'm sure he would, I'm pretty nearly damn certain he would; but I don't want him to. And when he's started, of course, it would make him angry if I made him stop, and it would not be fair, because I did lead him on, sexually I mean, I was the one who started it. I need him so much, I need him to stay with me and love me. He's like a god to me, he created me, I owe him so much – I was just a little tart in some San Francisco joint whose mother had been a hooker and who was going nowhere fast. He made me alive, he made me feel, and all that feeling is for him.

Of course sometimes when he's out I remember just how bloody stupid it is. What's the point of being halfway across the world if you have to stay in your room the whole time?

What's the point of getting top billing and making a fortune if you never see a cent of it? But he comes in and he wants me to be happy and waiting and ready for him, and if I'm not he's so disappointed and knotted up and sad that he can't control himself. It's because he loves me and wants me so much that he gets so angry. I've set his feelings free, he says: before he met me he was all cold, screwed up tight and ungiving, because his mother was a frigid bitch who never gave him any loving, but now I've set all his feelings free, all of them, his loving and his anger and his sadness and his danger, and I must accept them all. Together, he says, we have crashed the barriers of dreary old morality; together we have been set free to understand and enjoy the utter, unutterable beauty of experience. And I know, I know it's true because he has done that for me too. So how can I spit out all my old childish loneliness and jealousy and spite at him, when he takes me in his arms and my belly moves and sings for him, and for him alone? When I know that what we play-act twice nightly before an audience of thousands is true: he took me out of nothing, he destroyed my old life, the old me, he chopped it up in little bits and threw them all away and then he remade me all himself. I do not exist without him. He made me, he can destroy me, that's his right, and it is all right with me.

I don't mind him going out so much, anyway. I don't even like the friends he has now, I don't know them or understand them and they probably wouldn't like me. They're all so fine and fancy, and clever and smart. When we were still in America we went out a lot, especially in New York – we had fun together and good friends. Mostly vaudeville people, and we were all doing well and there was champagne and parties and a car and decent restaurants and pretty clothes. They were all just people like us, who were suddenly pleased with ourselves and finding the good time after quite a long lot of looking, in some cases. It was lovely, actually; everyone knew who you were really so they didn't mind you pretending to be better than you were, and they were pretending with you.

But after we got to Berlin he started changing. He was an Indian all the time, and he wanted me to be one too. He read mad books at night and started saying he could see the future, started telling me about his powers. He became a stranger and only in bed could I bring him back to me, and only then if I was willing to follow him wherever he wanted to go. He went out late at night drinking absinthe with young men who weren't like us at all. Wild hairy young students and they could talk up a storm. It was quite exciting to listen to at first. I was heady with it, and by all the words they knew and how they treated us – well him, and me with him – as their equals. And they knew so much stuff: poets and thinkers and political writers and strings and strings of wonderful crazy words. They seemed wonderfully romantic to me, though silly too and often rather sweet, though I knew better already than to tell them so. They thought they were so dangerous and splendid. They were delightfully against morality, and I didn't like to tell them they were saying nothing that every pro on the waterfront has known for too long and wants to forget. They told him that experience was beautiful, only experience was pure, pure for its own sake. They thought they should prepare themselves for pure experience, for its fullness and its richness, by giving up all the old rules, morality and manners and conventions and stuff; that nothing mattered, that all those things got in the way. I could smile thinking of him and me together in our bed and how that was true and how exciting it was to have thrown away the rules and be in Berlin pretending to be an Indian and getting rich. But I couldn't take them seriously.

Then one night they started asking him about India and his god and his vision of the world and how they could purify themselves and master their emotions through sacrifice and yoga like he did. I started to giggle and he was furious. I thought he would think it was funny, but he didn't see the joke. That's the sort of thing I meant when I said he was starting to believe his whole act. He told me truth was one more convention that had to be set aside, and so was my mockery for the emergence of his true personality. He told me that he was a great master and that lower beings might need truth but he did not. And he meant it. I was really frightened for a bit – I thought maybe he was cracking up. But the act went on being good, he never put a finger wrong. I should have put my foot down, then and there, but he was so happy and so nice when I agreed with him and so fierce when I didn't. So I didn't. But on the other occasions he would talk of his own friends with so much scorn, so coldly; he would laugh at them and say they were dross for his use, silly fools with words but no wisdom. But they were only foolish little boys.

In Paris, wonderful Paris that I had dreamed of, Paris where I bought lovely dresses and hats that he would not let me wear, in Paris it was more of the same, but different somehow. More spinning words and too much booze, but his friends there took drugs and he did too. And he started to sleep with other women and come home to me and boast about it to me. And worse, somehow, the way he spoke about those women, the way he would mock and jeer at them, talk filth about them to me, foul, disgusting sneering at the poor things. Then he wanted me to sleep with other men and tell him about them; he wanted me to do things with other men, and other women, and have him watch us. When I said it was wrong he hit me – not for fun, not for sex, but hard cold in anger; it was the first time he had ever done that. He knocked me to the floor and stood over me and said there was slave morality and master morality and if I chose to be a slave he would treat me like one, but if I wanted to be a free spirit I must obey him. I told him I couldn't help my natural feelings and he stood over me, tall and beautiful, and he said, and I can remember it clearly, he said natural feelings were only there to challenge the striving soul. 'I am showing you the Superman,' he said sternly. 'Natural man is something that can be overcome, that must be surpassed.' And I was so frightened and so crazy for him and he was so completely filled up with his own power that I said I wanted to be his slave, the slave girl of the new Superman, and he smiled. I thought about running away then, when I said it, and bloody well should have too. After that it was too late. Once I had accepted his smile, consented to it and to what followed that smile; once I had learned how far he was prepared to go with my body and how I was prepared to follow him there, how I could love what he did to me and cry out for more, then there was no place to run. He was my whole world. Without him I did not exist. I love him most terribly.

And here in London, well, I don't see him much after the show. Late at night, in the early foggy mornings of London city, he comes in wild and hectic. I wait for him, sometimes all night, long past any desire to sleep, I wait for his hands and his teeth and his tongue to come to me and make me alive again, to take away the fear and the loneliness, to make me real, to make me feel. Occasionally his friends will come to the dressing room between the shows. Last night a long thin woman came; and she bowed low over his hand and called him Master and Guru. He smiled at her with infinite cold distance. I suppose I should have been glad of the distance. She petted me like I pet our little dog. She told me I was lucky to share my life with the life of the greatest spiritual master of our generation, but she was not speaking to me. She was speaking to him. He smiled. She smiled. As she left she reminded him, with caressing veneration, that she would see him later and was looking forward to a further display of his mystic powers. But that time she was talking to me and not to him.

And after she had gone I was glad that he hit me, that he beat me carefully and systematically where it hurt most and showed least, because it still meant that he needed me for something, just like I needed him.

Last night he raged on about the Superman. He told me that to find greatness a man must commit himself completely to his worldly goals, that he must be prepared to sacrifice life itself for them, and that out of the rubble, the ashes, the chaos of that destruction, that sacrifice, the Superman, the new all-powerful master of the universe, would arise. Then he went out and did not return all night.

And suddenly I knew what I had in fact known all along, known ever since we came to Europe. I will be the sacrifice. One day, one evening, under the glow of the stage lights he will cover me with the cloak and the lacquer lid and he will, in front of a breathless audience, a doting venerating crowd, he will cut me up into little bits with his long curved sword. He will be ecstatic while he does it. And the funny thing is, so will I. I won't roll away off the little table as I'm meant to do, slipping out under the concealed flap and dropping the dummy hand as I go. I'll take it, proud and happy and sexy. It will be wonderful. He will be the most powerful man in the world for that moment. He'll be the big star of the season. Their horror will be his ultimate reward and mine too. I'm the showman of this team and I always have been. It will be an unforgettable night at the theatre, I can tell you. And I don't mind too much, to tell the truth, because there is not much else left for me, and because I'm the only woman in the world he could do that to. I just want to let everyone else know first, because there's a bit of me, brought up to be a competent and capable hooker, who knows perfectly well that the whole thing is bloody stupid.

I don't know which night it will be. That's part of the magic.

But it will happen, one night.

I know. He knows I know. We have both known for quite a long time.

That is the extraordinary extra something that goes on stage with us each night. That's why the papers call it the 'most romantic act in town'.

It's a terrific act, though I say so myself.

MAYBE A LOVE POEM FOR MY FRIEND

— ❧ —

My friend has greying hair, a dangerous temper and tea breaks when she's working.

My friend has two sons and a secret man she keeps in a drawer and lets me peek at sometimes.

My friend writes poems that are witty, fierce and sometimes soppy.

My friend has funny jokes, a stream of gossip and standards so high that I need crampons.

My friend is the only person in the whole world that I am prepared not to smoke around, in the long term and without being asked. My friend wheezes sometimes which is alarming. She keeps a private space to disappear in and never prods at mine.

My friend and I wrote a book together. A quite different intimacy from lovers, and rarer.

My friend came round one day and saw my baby, so new that the birth-dust brought from his star-travelling was still fresh on him. It is a time when women have their families about them and she was mine.

My friend says, 'You should write poetry.' I answer, 'Does this count?'

THE TALE OF THE VALIANT DEMOISELLE

❦

I fingered the winterkilled grass, looping it round the tip of my finger like hair, ruffling its tips with my palms. Another year has twined away, unrolled and dropped across nowhere like a flung banner painted in gibberish. There is death in the pot for the living's food, fly-blown meat, muddy salt and plucked herbs bitter as squill. If you can get it. How many people have prayed for their daily bread and famished? In a winter famine, desperate Algonquian Indians ate broth made of smoke, snow and buckskin, and the rash of pellagra appeared like tattooed flowers on their emaciated bodies – the roses of starvation; and those who died, died covered in roses. Is this beauty, these gratuitous roses, or a mere display of force? Or is beauty itself an intricately fashioned lure, the cruellest hoax of all?
Annie Dillard, *Pilgrim at Tinker's Creek*

'Mummy, Billy says I can't play soldiers with him because I'm a girl.'

'Well, don't play soldiers then, it's a silly game.'

'Mummy.' Exasperation, frustration, an answer not good enough.

'Well then, tell him not to be so silly, tell him you're Thérèse Figueur.'

'Who's she?'

'She was a soldier in the freedom army of the French

47

Revolution. And later the great General Bonaparte himself gave her a medal.'

(But don't tell her because eight is too young to know, don't tell her that on campaign in 1799 the Piedmontese peasants demanded that she should be given over to them, to be burned as a witch. And her comrades in arms consented.)

'Mummy, Billy says I can't be Robinson Crusoe 'cause he was a man; I have to be Man Friday all the time.'

'That doesn't make sense.'

Yes it does, of course. Her own son. Oh, Christ.

'Tell him that there was a woman castaway over a century before Alexander Selkirk – he was the true man that Defoe made up Robinson Crusoe from. She was called Marguerite de la Rocque, and she was so brave that the Queen of Navarre put her into one of the first books of stories that was ever written in France.'

(But don't tell her, because eight is too young to know, that Marguerite of Navarre, sister of Francis the First, the most sophisticated, intelligent and virtuous woman in all Europe, had to lie, had to change the story, had to make it respectable, and had to present her whole courage as coming from her love of a man.)

'Mummy, tell me that story.'

Over four hundred years ago Columbus sailed across the Atlantic and discovered America. Then the Spanish and the Portuguese went there and they brought back lots of exciting stories and lots of gold.

(And they killed and raped the Indians and destroyed their culture, and paid for their gold with measles and syphilis; but don't tell her that bit because she is too young to have to know.)

So then the people in England and France got a bit jealous and they thought they'd like to find some new countries too, and gold and spices and silk and adventures, so they built ships and set out. And one of the first to set out was a sailor from St Malo, in Brittany, and his name was Jacques Cartier. He made two voyages, wild and difficult journeys beyond the end of the world. You must understand how brave you had to be to go to the strange countries across the Atlantic which might not even exist: a few fishermen had gone before to fish on the Great Banks where the cod ran so fat and plentiful that they could be pulled up for the asking if you could make the crossing; but Cartier went beyond that, he sailed his little ship into a new sea, a new ocean, and he thought he had found the way across the top of the world and through to China. Actually, though, he'd found the Gulf of St Lawrence which leads into the Canadian interior. Some Indians he met told him that if he could travel up the great river he would come to a magic land called Saguenay, where there was gold and jewels and strange beautiful things, and people with one leg, and unicorns and spice trees. He spent one winter up the St Lawrence river, where Quebec is now, and no one from Europe had ever seen such cold, so much snow, such hard frosts; and they got scurvy and other diseases and the river was full of rapids; so he realised that if they were going to explore this new country and find Saguenay they would have to build a base, found a colony there on the river as a sort of launching pad for the interior. So he went home and asked the King of France to give him money and ships and people to go and found a city in New France. The King thought this was a very good idea, but he was a bit of a snob and he didn't think that Cartier, who was just a master mariner and captain, was the right person to be in charge of a new country. So he appointed another man, who was a nobleman called Jean François de la Rocque, Sieur de Roberval, to be Lieutenant General and in charge of everything. But of course Cartier knew more about it all and was better at getting organised than Roberval, so he set out first with about half the people and equipment they needed, and he built the fort and spent another freezing depressing winter in Canada; but at the end of the winter Roberval still hadn't turned up, and they thought he wasn't coming, and so many of the company had died and they were all fed up, so Cartier decided to go home.

In the meantime Roberval had finally got his act together, but I don't think he really had very much idea about what exploring was really like, because he took a very strange expedition, including lots of ladies and gentlemen who were friends of his, as well as sailors and soldiers and working people. And for the grand people it was all like an exciting adventure, a picnic almost; they didn't have the least idea about how dangerous and wild Canada really was. And one of the ladies who went was his own niece, a pretty young woman, about eighteen, called Marguerite, which means both a daisy and a pearl in French.

Imagine it; they sailed out of La Rochelle harbour in the spring winds of April, three ships with their square sails set and their high castles at the front and back. There were three hundred soldiers, sixty masons and carpenters, ten priests, three doctors, and all sorts of necessary stuff, like pre-fab carts to put together when they got there, and mills and ironware. And all the crowds of La Rochelle stood on the harbour and cheered and sang to see such a brave expedition going off under the King's Lieutenant General to discover and conquer a New World. They had a safe and sunny crossing of the huge Atlantic and arrived in the harbour at Newfoundland; and they must all have felt very happy and confident.

But then, while they were resting in the harbour and in such high spirits, Cartier sailed in and told them that it would be impossible to defend themselves against the cold and the Indians, and that he for one was going home to

France; his crew wouldn't face another Canadian winter and it was all Roberval's fault for not arriving when he had said he would. Roberval was really the commander officially, but Cartier was older and more experienced, and it was probably difficult for him to take orders from Roberval. Because, when Roberval ordered him to stay and return to the St Lawrence, Cartier took his three ships and stole away at night and sailed back to France.

I expect that everyone in Roberval's expedition was really upset by this, and probably a bit frightened as well. They had come all this way thinking that Canada would be a rich country littered with gold and jewels for them to pick up and have some good adventures on the way, but they must all have known that Cartier was the most knowledgeable sailor and explorer in all France and if he said it was impossible then . . .

Then the excitement and the tension would have mounted. The mutterings, fear and anger, and their dreadful, dreadful dependence on Roberval, now not the golden young lord from Picardy who had friends at court and wit and charm, but an iron man, a despotic arrogant young man who could not take advice from anyone. And wanting comfort, wanting fun, wanting reassurance . . . and he was so pretty, so gallant and young and fine, and his wife was so far away and perhaps they would never go home, perhaps they would freeze to death and die here in the strange country. And it was high spring and the bright salty air filled with sea birds in the May sunshine.

Perhaps they would never go home because they had come to the New World beyond the dangerous ocean, where the old harsh laws did not apply and they were young and beautiful. Of course she had an affair with him, sneaking down among the bales and goods in the lower hold, sneaking away with him across the rocky beaches where the sea birds were nesting too. His face so salty under his beard and her legs so white under her petticoats. To make love in the New World where even the stars

51

were different. And when the company sailed on again, how could they stop? Roberval's gentlemen volunteers were a young and brave band, unconventional, high-spirited. Their lines of decorum shifting, what was and what was not allowed. And, dear God, how she wanted him; couldn't keep her hands to herself, in those cramped close quarters and nowhere to get away. Just to see him toss his curls, his ear-rings dancing, made such shivers in her belly. She had to touch him. And when she touched him it was not enough, and there was no retreat. The sweetness of first love. She was crazy about him, greedy for him, lost her good sense, lost her good name, and three-quarters of the below-decks crew must know about it, the Governor's own niece, because there was so little space and it could not be kept secret.

So probably everyone was a little nervous and edgy when they sailed on. They went up the coast of Newfoundland and into the Gulf of St Lawrence through the Strait of Belle Isle. In the summer time it is stunningly beautiful – flocks of sea birds, great plunging gannets, little funny puffins, and seals disporting themselves under the cliffs of little rocky islands and to the north the low flat lands of Labrador and Quebec stretching away away endlessly into the unknown places. We don't exactly know what happened, but Marguerite did something that upset Roberval very badly and he refused to have her on his ship any longer. They were passing some little islands at the time – they're called the Harrington Islands now, they're quite little but luckily for her they have some fresh water – and he put her on one of them and sailed on.

Why could he not forgive her? Dear God, she had wept and sought forgiveness, crawled on her knees to him. She knew, she knew damn well, he was a Calvinist, a hard man wedded to his Bible, but . . . but he was willing to forgive her lover, and that hurt. It was she, she alone, who was damned; had gone outside his and his God's forgiveness. In the July sunshine the island looked pretty enough; it was not that. She could not read the meaning on her uncle's face. He could not forgive her, and he said it was God's judgement. He said they sailed with God and he would keep no blighting Jonah on his ship, no whores. He needed to show his power over them all. He could not stomach her beauty, her joy; she was radiant with her love, love flowered her flesh rosy and the sun and the sea flowered it golden. She was too beautiful for him to forgive her. He would, he said, have no befouling lust on his ship; but he was willing to keep her lover. It was woman flesh that stuck in his craw. She was the Gateway to Hell, and his gallant young men must not risk her corruption. A whore, a slut, a witch out of hell.

So he gave her few provisions and sailed on westwards towards central Canada.

He gave her a gun, he gave her a flintbox, he gave her a Bible.

Cartier had made a list, a list of the minimum supplies necessary to survive – 276 men, including apothecaries, tailors, carpenters, masons, blacksmiths, men-at-arms. He had written his list for the King saying they would need windmills, boats, anvils, food supplies, bales of woollen cloth, artillery, domestic animals and hens, geese, seeds, grain, cooking utensils and pig-iron. They had all known the list and laughed at some of the meticulous details, and they had felt safe because Cartier knew his job.

He gave her a gun, a tinderbox and a Bible.

He wanted her dead.

He didn't want her blood on his hands.

He said if she was so damn free she could taste the freedom of the savages.

She had asked him for sugar and he had hit her in the face.

She did not know how to use the gun. He gave ammunition and powder, but he knew she did not know how to use the gun. One of the sailors putting her ashore gave her his own knife. It was a kindness, but when he slipped it to her he was careful not to let his hand touch hers. He set his mouth in silent embarrassment. The whole ship's company was embarrassed, but silent. No one raised a murmur for her. One of the priests had raised his hand to bless her and thought better of it. She was in mortal sin. She did not repent.

But just as the ship was sailing away her . . . her boyfriend leapt over the side and came swimming to the shore; he had decided to stay and help her.

The silly fool. The silly beautiful fool; his arms so long and white, cutting the smooth surface of the bay. His grin irrepressible, his body glorious. She went down into the water to welcome him as he swam towards her, standing almost to her waist in the soft sea, her arms stretched out. And there, in the sight of the ship's company, they fell into each other's arms giggling, laughing. For those few moments she had felt so bereft, she had felt the taste of loneliness and death and he had leapt into the sea to come to her. Holding hands they ran up the shingle, dripping wet, her dress clinging to her legs, his shirt clamped on his chest revealing his nipples. This was their paradise; they could fuck all day. Morality had abandoned them, they were free. Outrageous, bold, untrammelled, they waved handkerchiefs to the departing boat, laughing.

Then they lived very happily for a while. They built a hut out of the pine trees, out of logs, and they made furniture for it and got it all as cosy as they could, just like in *Robinson Crusoe* and *Swiss Family Robinson* – well, almost like; it couldn't have been so good, because they didn't have those handy wrecks the others had to get supplies off – they didn't have nails for instance, so the hut can't have been very secure. And an island in the Gulf of St Lawrence is rather a different thing from a warm sunny one in the Caribbean. But luckily Marguerite was very clever and creative, and she sewed and carved and made fishing lines by unravelling her petticoats; and her boyfriend shot and fished and they ate berries and fruit and stuff like that. It was hard work, but they did have a lot of fun.

At first. It was their paradise. Each morning she woke snuggled in the curve of his armpit. They played and teased and laughed and made love through a long golden summer, and at night the stars were heavy and golden; bigger brighter newer stars than they had ever seen, and they named new constellations in the honour of their loving. And she knew she was going to have his baby. It was their paradise and they giggled together and swore they would never eat the apple of civilisation again; and that when Roberval came back to rescue them they would laugh in his face and tell him to sail away wherever he wanted for they were content. The sun shone warmly and she grew lean and fit and free in her limbs as she had never been since childhood, and they wandered their kingdom naked and unashamed as the savages were said to do.

But. Except. There was an undertow. A darkening shadow. The sex was not as good as it had been on ship board: there was nothing else to do, nothing to hide, nothing to plot, no planning, no scheming, no exciting delays. And he: he thought he had been so wonderful, so heroic and generous and romantic, leaping off the ship for her. He acted, just, at moments, hardly hinted, barely noticed in the delight of sunshine, he acted as though she owed him something. But Roberval would have forgiven him, would have kept him on the ship. Sometimes she thought that he, somehow, somewhere, agreed with Roberval – and yet what had she done that he had not? He thought that by forgiving her he had earned her love. She would give it to him as a gift, but not as a debt. But she did not like to say these things and intrude on their happy laughter. And when the evenings began to be cooler and longer she found that his conversation was not very interesting to her, and she started even to read the Bible to amuse herself, and he resented it and she felt guilty.

In Canada, you know, the autumns are extraordinary. They had never seen anything like it, that wild extravagance of colour; none of that soft mournful wet decline that we have here in Europe but golds and yellows and crimsons and scarlets after the first frost. There's a time they call the Indian Summer, St Martin's Summer, late in October, when the winds die down and the days are hot and hazy, and they must both have felt that all was well with them and that the rumours about the winter had been a mistake, a silly joke. Perhaps they played that they were a king and queen who had ordered one of the new Italian artists to come and decorate their palace for them, in the bright, brave, gaudy colours of that time.

And then the winter came.

Cold. She had not known what the word meant. They had been warned and like children they had not heard the warning, because they had no knowledge or experience to measure the warning against. Early one dawn the calm had been broken by a whirring noise, a low murmur with an inner beat, an unearthly sound. The heavy skeins of geese were passing, straight as arrows, running south and pulling the darkness of winter down on their strong pinion feathers from the north. She thought of the baby and she was frightened. And they went, innocent and ignorant as children, into the maelstrom of winter. Hell would not be hot, but cold and everlasting as that Canadian winter: and the weight of the snow drift, drift, drifting forever, or born on the storm winds, battering out of the north; the bay rearing up against them, iced spume far flung; the great reefs of ice riming up along the shore, shifting and moaning like hellish harps at first, but as the cold locked down tighter there came an ominous and enormous silence in which there was no noise at all but the relentless wind. How could she help thinking about the baby and being frightened? The fear moved in, gnawing as fierce as the cold, and there was no escape from either. And the hut itself a feeble joke before the cold and the wind and the terror. Hunger. Thirst. Tedium and the smoky darkness of their frail shelter. The immense heart-breaking effort that the simplest task of survival used up. The weariness. And above and beneath and within all things, the numbing, bemusing, battering cold. And in the hut with nothing to do they tried to keep warm, clinging together not for delight, or for tenderness, or even for consolation, but for need – a need more gripping and impelling than the need of their lust in the far away and almost forgotten springtime. And the bitterness of the need crept in between them and wedged itself there and there was nothing, nothing left at all of the golden loving but a bitter cringing hatred and a bitterer and more cringing need.

And then I'm sorry to say, that winter her boyfriend died.

She killed him. She was both whore and murderess. The bitterness had eaten them up and they snapped and snarled still locked together against the cold. Like bears in a den. Fire in them both, fires flaring for no reason, and violent savage sex afterwards that used energy and did not restore affection. And when he hit her, when he started hitting her, she grovelled before him, begging, pleading with him to stop, apologising for things she had never done and of which he had not even accused her, cradling her belly and her head, rolling on the ground, crawling before him on hands and knees, begging, beseeching, pleading. She hated him more for reducing her to that humility than she hated him for hitting her. She hated him and herself and they had come to a great black place from which neither could escape.

Finally she had turned, turned on him for no real reason beyond the cold and her sordid humiliation. She had half broken the hut apart in the cataclysm of her fury, hurling abuse and objects and spit and spite: savage, animal, rodent, vicious. And where was the young and tender girl who had stood on the deck of the ship out of La Rochelle and longed to see the glories of the New World? She drove him in her mad anger out of the hut and into the wind. He was weak, confused by the cold and by her raving. He slipped. He gashed his leg. Hours later, frozen and blue-lipped, he crawled back into the hut. It had not seemed a bad wound at first, though quite deep, about two inches above his ankle. She resented him; resented shredding yet more of her inadequate clothing to bind the wound. She resented his clumsiness and the extra burden it laid on her. She resented her own guilt and the skill with which he had punished her. A few days later when she took off the bandage to re-dress the wound, she noticed that it was opening up, high and proud, and that the

57

flesh above was puffy, greenish. He could put no weight on the foot. It was not getting better. A sweet, sticky smell pervaded the hut. Two nights later she heard the foxes howling outside and in the morning their marks were around the door. The skin above the bandage turned black. He had a fever, muttering through the night while the wild beasts howled. In his fever he said dreadful things, about her, about himself and about Hell. She knew that he was telling the truth. It took him three weeks to die.

She tried to dig him a grave, but the ground was too hard. She dragged his body into a snowdrift and it took all the strength she had. In the night she heard the foxes again, excited, with greedy snufflings and snarls. When she went out they were like white ghosts pawing and pulling at his corpse. She frightened them away and knew they would return. She dragged the body back into the hut and collapsed beside it. All night long she held him in her arms, rocking him and herself in a fever of passion. God how she loved him, how beautiful he was, how long and strong in the shadows, his skin so soft and sweet. She had loved him and sacrificed her life for him. He had betrayed her and deserted her. He had run away and left her, dishonoured and pregnant, cast out from society, alone in the wilderness, pregnant, alone and bitter. It was an old boring story, a woman's story, and she had thought herself to be above it. God how she hated him, and there was no love so sweet as this loathing, a hatred so strong that it warmed her at last. It enflamed her, she kissed his body all over, everywhere, long hard kisses, and she buried her lips in his gangrenous wound, tasting and probing the putrid flesh. He was dead. She was alone.

All that winter she guarded his body in the hut. She no longer minded the smell. The white foxes still came at night, waiting, waiting, waiting their chance. When she did not hear their shrill barking, she heard the deep and dreadful howling of the wind, tearing across the water, across the ice. Beating against the hut, seeking access, seeking her flesh with a wild lust that would not be tamed by her. And in the ghastly screaming of the wind, she heard a voice she could not hear, words she did not know. The hut was too small; she could not step away from him; his body bloated up, his lips pulled away from his blackened gums into a grin of malevolent triumph. He swelled larger and larger and she did too. But he was dead and she was alive. She ceased to care.

At last there came a day which felt different, though she could not tell what the difference was; an ending, a beginning, a changing. Outside it was as cold as ever, but along the rim of the horizon far away as she could see there was a separation: between slate-grey water and slate-grey sky there was a rim of pale pink. She gathered snow and melted it. She stripped off her clothes and washed herself. She covered his face with a rag: there were things that no man, alive or dead, should see.

She was in labour for thirty-three hours and there was no one to wipe the sweat from her face; it clogged her eyes, matted her hair and trickled salty into her mouth, and when night came she was wrapped in a shroud of ice. She screamed and heard in her own howls the echoes of the waiting foxes. She was animal. She crawled on the hut floor and chewed pieces of wood. She smashed at her own body. The pain threw her around the hut and shook her as a dog shakes a rat, and in the teeth of the pain she became a rat and snarled like a rat. And she screamed to him for help and he could not help her because she had killed him. She was far away from the places where there are other people. Then later she was weary, weary, weary with the pain and the loneliness, and there was no one to bring her vinegar on a sponge.

Just before the spring came she had her baby, all on her own in that little hut. It's very hard work for a woman to have a baby, and you really need to have people with you to help you and hold on to you. She must have been terribly brave to go through that all on her own.

Out beyond the place of courage, of choice, of free will, she came at last to chasm, enormous and black, and she knew that it could not be endured any longer and she lay down on the floor almost quietly to await the end. She knew her body would be ripped apart by the devil flesh in it, and particles of her would be caught in the evil wind and hurled in flayed fragments across the island, out on to the icecap, and lost for ever in the great white desert. And then, miraculously, she found a new strong rhythm, and she leaned on the rhythm and recognised in it some of the rhythm of her desire and it was the sweet rhythm of passion which had brought her to this last place. But it was a new place too, a new command, a new power, a new dignity. And she pushed down, bracing herself firmly against the wall of the hut. She was no longer herself, but a new strong woman, and not cold, nor hunger, nor death itself could stop her in the power of her striding. She would walk the great white plains beyond the ocean, beyond the sunset, and give birth to a child in the New World. And in the first shadow turning of the morning her daughter was born, tiny, white, bloody and screaming defiance and joy and life. And never, never, since the dawn of days, had anything been more beautiful and she was no longer alone and the spring would come with the child and they would blossom and flourish like the bay tree. She wrapped her tiny daughter as warmly as she could and they lay together watching the light creep into the hut, creep into the world, and she was filled with a fierce triumphant joy.

But sadly the baby died.

There wasn't any milk. The baby sucked and sucked and sucked. White and little and eager. At first it seemed to grow and strengthen, responding to the promise of spring and to her enormous, welcoming love. Soon, soon, the spring would come, the snow would melt and there would be growing things and she would stop bleeding and go out and hunt and put on weight and both the land and her breasts would flow with milk and wild honey, and the child would be the first daughter of freedom. But there was no milk. And she was too tired, too tired, too tired. So for six weeks she watched the baby die, its huge wise eyes uncomplaining, its tiny mouth still trusting, still hoping, still sucking. It shrank, shrivelled away just as the snow was doing, and suddenly in the middle of one night she knew that it was dead.

It could have hung on a little longer, just a little longer. Just a few days later from far away on the mainland she heard the gonging of the breaking ice and very soon she was able to bury them together, and with the burial it was springtime, and small white flowers blossomed among the rocks and the sea birds laid their eggs casually in the crevices of the cliffs. Then the great geese flocks pulled the warm weather with them as they flew northwards overhead to their nesting grounds. They passed so thickly that using the gun for the first time she was able to have roast goose for supper every night for weeks and the fat ran down her chin sweet and oily. She could not bear to think about her little white baby, so she did not. She had survived and the sun came out sweetly and warmed the cold marrow in the depths of her bones.

So that when the spring came she was all on her own and she must have felt that she would never get off the island. She could see other islands not too far away and on clear days probably the mainland too low in the distance, but she had no way of getting that far; probably she did not even know how to swim, because rich girls in those days weren't taught that sort of thing, but even if she could, why should she leave what little she had to go to another deserted island? That corner of eastern Quebec is, even today, one of the most godforsaken places in the world; there are still no towns, no roads, no nothing, just spruce trees and silver birches and scrub and rocky land for miles and miles and miles northwards until you get to the Arctic. Southwards was the great sea, reaching as far as she could see, and for all she knew it went on forever.

And perhaps this was really the time when her courage was most tested, when she was bravest of all. Because now she had no one depending on her, no one needing her like her baby did, no reason at all for keeping going. And she knew what it was really like; she knew there would be another winter, and another winter, and another winter, and she must often have wondered why she bothered at all. She must have been dreadfully lonely and desperate

61

and miserable sometimes, but she kept struggling on.

She had to learn how to do all sorts of new things – things that no woman she had ever heard of had done. She must have learned to shoot and fish and hunt, and build fires and find eggs, and chop wood. She even shot a couple of bears.

And in a different way that second year was worse than the first had been, partly because she wasn't so strong and well as she had been the year before. She really wasn't getting enough to eat, and especially not enough vegetables and greens, and she had had the baby which must have worn her down. But also something very scary began to happen to her: she was attacked by demons. Well, I expect really they were just in her head, and perhaps she was going a little crazy or something from being on her own for so long and not knowing if she would ever see another human being in her whole life; and because of the sad sad things that had happened to her. But she believed in them all right, and all through her second winter on the island they tormented her, howling round her little hut and scaring her out of her mind. She even tried to shoot them with her gun, but that didn't work at all.

Busy. Busy. It was essential to keep busy. To wake up in the morning and make plans, and then to carry them out. Be organised. Be efficient. Today I will find grasses and mosses and stuff the cracks in the hut walls; today I will walk across the island and watch the seals playing; today I will check the lines and lay them for fish.

In the spring she shot a bear; a big, rough, brown bear. She never knew where it had come from; she walked through the spruce trees one day and there it was, its back to her, grazing. Almost without thinking she shot it dead, and realised with a deep joy that she would have a warm cover for the next winter. The bear meat made her sick, she did not eat it; but she had skinned the fur off, hacking bloodily, excitedly through a whole day, the warm fur, the warm blood and the distant memories of the pig-killings at the childhood farm in Picardy. And she stretched the skin and dried it and salted it and scraped it and it was a great victory. She danced for herself on the green grass and thought that she was the only French lady in the whole world who had killed a bear and stretched its fur for a blanket. There were so many little joys. She had to think about them and keep busy. She danced for hours before she felt silly and naked and self-conscious. Naked, bloody and dancing like a savage; if she were not careful she would forget how to be a decent Christian; she added reading the Bible to her daily tasks.

That summer she thought she was happy. She did not let herself think about the things that made her unhappy. She did not sleep much for when she was asleep dreams came to her and they did not make her happy. She stayed up through the nights and watched the heavy stars and thought about nothing and sang little snatches of old songs, and of new ones that she made up for herself. And as autumn came she noticed with amusement that like the animals her hair was turning white for the winter.

What changed? It changed the day she shot the second bear.

She saw them from her hut, the great swimming bears, white and strong, churning up the channel to her little cove. A huge white bear, creamy and immense, black nose and mighty forelegs. And with it two bear cubs; half grown, snowier. She sat still by her hut and watched them enchanted. The mother bear stretched out and the little ones curled against her great wet flank and they dozed a little on the pebbles. Then the cubs woke up and they played, such joyful play, and so like children, rolling and cuffing and delighting, nose to nose the two cubs and heaving up over their mother's body while she stirred in her sleep and pushed them off with those great fierce paws made gentle in mother-love; and they nuzzled her and rollicked in the autumn sunshine while the sea reflected a soft, playful approval. She wanted desperately to go and play with them, rolling and smothering in that density of white fur, that warm and vital softness. And she knew that if she moved, if she coughed or stirred, they would be gone, back on a sudden into the sea and she would be alone again.

Then she knew in all her being that her baby was dead and that she was alone and the realisation broke her heart. And in a great anger of jealousy for the bear mother, of jealousy and spite, she glided, crafty, graceful – oh, yes, premeditated; made – not wild and manic in her jealousy – but mean, mean. She got her gun and she stood at the door of her hateful hopeless little hut and she shot one of the bear cubs. At the explosion the mother bear leapt up on to her hind legs and roared; and she thought for one glorious moment that the bear would come, terrible as the Lord on Judgement Day, and kill her dead, and she could go where her daughter had gone and be silent as stone for always and for ever more. And even as she thought that she was reloading her gun, ready, determined.

The mother bear looked at her baby, poked it with her nose, and then she and the other cub took to the sea, a great slither of white fur and hard muscle and they were gone. From the rocks beyond the cove she thought she could hear the wail of ursine grief, the great screams of a loving mother whose child has been stolen away by death. Slowly she went down the beach, slowly with her bare foot she touched the baby bear. It was not dead, it turned to her, its eyes pleading love. It was bigger than her baby, but white, white as an egg, and it had the same dark, puzzled, huge, wise eyes. Unthinking, she bunched her fist and put it on the cub's muzzle, and the bear sucked it firmly for a moment and then it died. She pulled it on to her lap. Sadly she stroked the thick white fur and she wept.

The soul of her daughter who had longed to live had travelled forth into the body of a bear cub because the thick soft fur would protect her from the cold. She had killed the mother bear's child and she had killed her own child. Everything that she touched she killed; his violence had not been in him, it had been in her. She had killed him. She had killed her daughter, and her daughter's soul had gone into the body of the bear, into the great rich womb of the mother bear and had come out safely again; her child's soul had found at last a real, a good, a mighty mother, but she had killed her child again.

So when the winter frosts came again she lay broken under the brown bear's fur, cuddling and caressing the fur of the small white bear, her daughter whom she had killed twice. And when the winds came the demons came too. She let them come. She gave them power. She let them come because with the white fur in her arms she could not refuse all the memories any more. For three weeks he had lain dying and she had hated him; she had killed him and she had hated him. For thirty-three hours she had laboured for her daughter, but it was not enough. The child had died and she had been there and had done nothing. She had not been able to save her. Slowly, cunningly she had crept into the hut, and taken the gun, and killed the snow-white bear, for no reason, no reason but spite and jealousy and greed for power.

The mother bear sent the demons.

The mother bear had come to the island to be her friend and guard, to let her burrow into that thick fur, to let her pass the winter curled up against the store of sweet fishy fat. And she had killed the mother's cub. The mother's child, her own child. So the mother bear had sent the demons.

No. The mother bear was a demon. She had come on the shoulder of the snow storm to torture her with memories.

God had sent the demons to punish her, because she had killed another woman's child, for spite.

God did not exist. God had abandoned her. God could not endure the hellish cold. Here, in this land, she had gone beyond the power of God. She had come into the power of demons. God who had hung on the cross had given her, in his weakness, over to the strength of the demons.

The demons came in from the sea as the mother had come. They came riding the wind, triumphant and screeching. They came on the driving eddies of the snow storm. They howled about her house, shaking the timbers and trying to get in.

Last winter she had known there were voices in the wind, but she had not heard their words. Now she could hear. Now she was open to them. Now she could not escape them.

Whore, they said, whore, slut, cunt, bitch. Adulterer, murderer, blasphemer. Whore, slut, cunt, witch.

They stripped her down to the bare bone.

The wages of sin are death. This is judgement. Yea, though you flee to the uttermost parts of the sea, we will find you. The wages of lust are death. There is no escape. The sweetness of your white skin in his arms; the sweet smell of putrefaction.

Whore, slut, cunt, bitch. Death is too easy for you. We bide our time. You hear our voices in the foxes singing for their carrion flesh. You stink of sin; they will not need to wait until you are dead.

You birthed us in the power you birthed your baby. You thought, you slut, that you were strong and free; in the maw of your stinking belly you gave birth to use. Your daughter is our mother. Her soul fled howling and angry to the north places and she bred us there. The daughter of sin, the child of adultery, bred demons and witches out of her tiny cunt. Monsters. We are your children.

Hairy, the Devil is hairy. Your gash is hairy. You let him put his foul, hairy member into yours. You encouraged him. You kissed the arse of the Devil and bound yourself to the demons. We are better lovers than he. You grovelled to him to tickle your slit. We will slit you, and you will grovel to us, beg, plead, whimper. Witch. Your uncle knew. A wise young man. Upright. Holy. Beloved of God. He was given the gift of discernment. He could smell your corruption and he rooted you out. He gave you to us because you deserved it. Whore.

They burn witches. The market places of Picardy are sweet with the smell of cooked flesh. We are burning you, burning you to the bone with cold and grief.

Humble yourself, daughter of pride. Grovel. Beg. Beg us. You begged him and we are stronger. Much stronger. Grovel to us or we will break you. We will break your body. We will break your mind.

Calmer moments: the bright freezing nights, when the rocking and the pounding of the hut remitted. She would step outside to breathe, and the sky would be illuminated with the strange cold fireworks from the north, a spectacle making nonsense of the night and of the winter and of her puny littleness in the whole great void beyond the west of the world. And then they would come again, the demons, whispering, singing sweet and low, women's voices, kind and gentle, luring her to a more secret doom: You can escape, once and for all, you can get away, sweetly, easily. Walk away from the hut, walk out into the snow, out into the sea and all will be well. They promised her insanity and suicide and made it a gift. They whispered on the brittle air that there was a place without pain, without sense or meaning, a place where dark and light, good and bad, cold and warmth were all the same and all indifferent. And even the shapes and sounds of words collapsed inwards, imploding, shaken in their fabric, breaking down, down, down into a warm place inside which there was no effort, no end, no beginning.

Come down, they murmured across the shapelessness of the flat sea, come down, come in, come closer. Come, come, come. A small step, an infinite drop, down, away, and the cold as sweet as a blanket and sleep, sleep, sleeeep. Dream a new time. A time before. Before there was anything; before the voice of God called the word of law across the void. When there was only the shapeless, wordless swirling. We can give you that, that formless, wordless rocking. We can give you that, if you submit. Let go. Submit. Bow down and worship us. Consent. You have only to consent. To let go.

And in the darkness she would cling to the frail hut, physically hold it, bite her own hands, hug the white fur until her ribs ached. She would remember, she would try to remember that the cold was a killer, that she must not leave the fireside. That spring came after winter, that order came out of chaos; and out of order came pattern and out of pattern history and life and herself. She did not consent. She did not submit. She was alive. She was still alive.

And then roaring again. Enormous. Fierce broken roaring. The noise so great it would break her ears open and her brains would strew the shore red on white. Slut. Whore. Cunt. SLUT. WHORE. CUNT. SSLLUUTTWWHHOORREECCUUN-NTT. Finished. You are finished, whore. We have the power here, cunt. We have the power and we will break you, slut. You are damned, whore; you are damned for all eternity. Damned, damned, Damned.

And on and on and on and on and on and on and on andon andon andon on on on on on on on on o n o n o n o n o n o nnnnnnnn oooooonnnnnnnn.

Until she cannot stand it any longer; and in a fury of destruction, anything, anything to silence their voices, she took the gun and shot at the wind through the roof, shoving in the shot, blasting wildly, great holes in the roof and powder burns on her arms and face. Bang, bang, bang. Enormous explosion – the wonderful great crashing of the gun at her behest silencing all other sounds, for a glorious and powerful time.

When the fury left her she saw she had used all her powder; there was none left. She had reached the end. She would die. And she lay on the floor of the hut, and their voices came again, no words now because she was as the animals are, just roaring and grunting and squealing and howling. How she had been in his arms. How she had been in her anger against him. How she had birthed her daughter. Pig grunts, and fox howls, and mewlings on her knees before his violence. And enormous growling, snarling, screeching and never never leaving her. And it was the end and all things were finished. And . . .

And no, she did not consent.

'I do not consent,' she said, and her own words echoed in the hut with a magnificent reality.

Words. Words at least were better. She seized the Bible. Grateful, even and suddenly, to Roberval who had given her nothing, but had not deprived her of human words, human contact.

> Out of the depths I have called unto you, O Lord; Lord hear my prayer. Oh let your ears consider well the voice of my complaint. If you, Lord, will be extreme to mark what is done amiss, Lord, who may endure it; but there is mercy with you and therefore shalt thou be feared.

And again louder. But their voices were louder still. WHORE. CUNT. SLUT. FOULNESS. ADULTERER.

> Then he said to the woman taken in adultery, Go in peace and sin no more. He said, Do not be afraid, be of good cheer, for behold I am with you always.

WITCH. SLUT. ANIMAL. IN THE SILENCE WE WILL KILL YOU. YOU ARE DAMNED.

And the Word was made flesh and dwelt among us.

WHORE. SLUT. WHORE.

And he blessed her saying, Much will be forgiven her, because she loved much.

BELIEVE THAT, FOOL, AND YOU'LL BELIEVE ANY-THING.

And when they had mocked him they stripped him. And they led him out to crucify him.

Whore. Slut. Cunt. Starving bag of bones, careened in the desert, lost, lost, hopeless.

It is when you are weak that you are strong.
God chose what is foolish in the world to shame the wise.
God chose what is weak in the world to shame the strong.

Witch. Slut. Whore. Your uncle deserted you, drove you out from the camps of men, gave you over to us.

And the Spirit drove him out into the wilderness. And he was in the wilderness forty days, fasting, tempted of Satan. He was with the wild beasts and the angels ministered to him.

Cunt.   Bitch.   whore.

He was with the wild beasts and the angels ministered to him. Do not be afraid, be of good cheer.
The word was made flesh.

We have power.

He was in the wilderness, fasting, and tempted of Satan.
He was with the wild beasts and the angels ministered to him.
Do not be afraid. Be of good cheer. For lo, I am with you always, even to the ends of the world.
I tell you, her sins which were many are forgiven, because she loved much.
I come that you may have life, and life more abundantly.

He was with the wild beasts and the angels ministered unto him.

silence.

The world was made flesh; and she wrapped him in swaddling bands and laid him in a manger because there was no room for them at the inn.

silence.

The word was made flesh and dwelt among us.

silence.

there was silence. And in the silence there was a turning of the year and in herself.

My soul magnifies the Lord, and my spirit rejoices in God my saviour;
God who is mighty has magnified me, and holy is His name. And all generations shall call me blessed.
He has put down the mighty from their seats and exalted the humble and meek. He has filled the hungry with good and sent the rich away empty.

it was an old song, a woman's song, a song of victory.

The winter was over. Naked, bloody, battered. Starving. She opened the door of the hut and fell forwards into the sunshine. The blood of battle stained her face. Emaciated, hanging on to life by a thin thread, the soft generosity of the white bear skin still in her arms. The roses of starvation flowering fresh on her back. She lay there, spread out. A deep and everlasting peace. To go so near to death that you have tasted its sweetness and decided against it. Decided for life. Hell had been harrowed, she had walked the unknown pathway and found the road home. Death had no more dominion.

Blessed are those who going through the valley of misery use it for a well, and the pools are filled with water. They

70

will go from strength to strength and unto the God of Gods appeareth every one of them in Zion.

It actually wouldn't matter if she died now.

But I shall not die, I shall live and praise my God.

She had been in the wilderness, fasting and tempted of Satan. But there were words spoken, fur coverings chanced upon, and a sunrise, a victory, a triumph. The silence in her head was perfect and perfectly peaceful.

And by amazing luck, after that winter was over, some Portuguese fishermen, driven in from the Great Banks, saw her fire smoke and came and rescued her. They took her back to France and she went home. Later she told her story to Jean Alfonce, who had been Roberval's pilot, and he told it to his friend and patroness Marguerite of Navarre, and she put it in her story book called the *Heptameron* and that's how we know about her.

'Mummy, what happened next?'

'She stayed in Picardy and taught school for the rest of her life.'

'Oh. Mummy?'

'Yes, darling.'

'Can I have a chocolate biscuit now?'

PROMISES

❦

'Darling.'

He was standing at the backdoor, calling.

She straightened up, gathered the branches from around her and came towards him. The contrast was too obvious: the solidness, the heavy gum boots, the square-framed, collapsed face, the badly cropped hair; and then the extravagantly ethereal quality of the branches she carried. Not ornamental cherry, rich and lusty, but odd irregular sprays of wild crabapple, pinkish white flowers, half-hearted almost, but so delicate. Japanese, he tried to think, but they weren't.

'Hello, old thing,' he said.

Don't call me that screamed her mind. 'Hello darling,' she said.

'Aren't you changed yet?'

'Changed?'

'O, come on, Chris, we're supposed to be over at the Vicarage in fifteen minutes.'

'I forgot.' She didn't say it apologetically, too much to bloody hope, he thought, it was a statement of fact, untrimmed like the rest of her. What was she thinking about?

Did I come all the way for this, she thought as she went upstairs pulling her jersey over her head. She often thought her thoughts in the words of the poetry she'd learned by heart in her nice girls'

73

school thirty years ago. Was it for this the clay grew tall . . . no, that was something else. Was it for this the clay grew tall? What was that?

She left the bedroom and went to the stair well. 'Henry?'

'Yes.'

'What's this: "Was it for this the clay grew tall?"'

A long pause. 'For God's sake, Chris, go and get dressed.'

But she knew by his tone that he was not angry with her for not being ready, but because he couldn't place her quotation. She unzipped her skirt and noticed his clothes all over the floor. Was it for this the clay grew tall? She felt depressed. She remembered the next line: 'What made fatuous sunbeams toil to break earth's sleep at all?' What, indeed; was it for this? This going to drinks at the Vicarage, this being called old thing. Was it for this that she had been made a ward of court, that she had eloped at seventeen and run off to Scotland to marry her penniless artist? The square-framed face had a madonna quality then, an air of serene courage. How romantic, her friends had said. Loving him she had been serving Art. Did I come all the way for this? Not actually to part at last without a kiss, but to endure the slow days of boredom, to endure the easy assumptions he made about her. He would have said and meant that he did not want her to make herself into a slave for him, but, subtle, insidious, the claim that he must be free to paint, that she did not serve him, but a higher good, Beauty, Art. What it meant was always being the one who picked up the clothes on the floor. And bigger things; to live in this pathetic provincial town, not to have children, not to interrupt, not to allow interruptions. So that he could paint pictures which made him slightly richer than the average bank manager, about as comfortable and bourgeois as the average solicitor, and all the while prating about the freedom, the wideness of space needed for Creation – which meant leaving his clothes lying about for her to pick up and being allowed, as ordinary men weren't any more, to say, laughingly but with hidden pride, that he didn't know how to boil an egg.

Wilfred Owen. What made the fatuous sunbeams toil to break earth's crust at all? *Futility*. A silly poem. If anything can wake him now, the kind old sun must know. The moment of delight, not seeing, but touching the crocus in the garden, just before he called. Poor Dorothy Wordsworth, she thought, her mind a thousand miles from the Vicarage drinks or Wilfred Owen. She was in the same boat as me, worse for her, she didn't even get . . . She reached for her blue wool dress, pulling it on to cover the blush that was spreading across her shoulders. Funny, while everyone else's embarrassment about sex was disappearing hers seemed to grow. Once she had stood in front of her parents. 'I shall have to marry him you know?' 'Have to, don't be silly.' 'Because he's my lover.' It hadn't been defiant, even if she had been only sixteen. It had been a simple statement of the facts. He's my lover. But now, in the privacy, as they say, of her own chamber, blushing as she had never blushed as a school girl. Why? Because it had come to be so important, to be the one constantly rich rewarding experience of her life, the thing that made it all almost worth it? She scrabbled for her lipstick and couldn't find it in the chaos of his creative activities in the bedroom. She didn't even like his pictures. She did find her shoes and dismissed the lipstick. Who was going to care? No discipline. No discipline of line. The lineaments of satisfied desire. But that desire was satisfied, damn Blake, it wasn't that she desired in her man. Control, his pictures lacked control. She wasn't a romantic any longer. She had grown up.

'Chris!'

'Coming, darling.'

She couldn't find her hairbrush either. She ran downstairs.

'Your hair is a mess.'

Does he think I'm a child? Damn him. He's meant to be the artist, not to care about brushed hair. She put her head against his breast; he picked up a brush from the hall table and began to brush the scruffy short hair on her neck. Perhaps he had meant it lovingly, a desire to touch her and groom her like happy monkeys. 'I love you,' she said, noticing with guilt that she only said it on those occasions when it was least true; when she needed to hear it, a despairing affirmation.

She wanted to pause there, leaning against him, but he pushed her chin up and brushed the front tufts.

'It's a mess,' he said again, and this time he meant a mess

75

beyond that which he could do anything about. 'We can afford to have it done properly, you know.'

'I'm used to it,' she said.

When they were first married and had no money, she'd nagged at him to let her have it done. 'I like it splayed out on the pillow,' he'd say. One day in a fit of temper on finding a hair in his soup he'd cut it off himself, hacking through it with the breadknife. And then he'd started to cry, weeping bitterly. How romantic, her friends said, envious: their husbands didn't get up at three in the morning to paint pictures and stay in bed till three in the afternoon to make love. They got up at eight to make money and sometimes stayed up till midnight to paint the bathroom. You can't say to people how romantic to have your bathroom painted for you.

'I can't go to the hairdressers,' she said now. 'It's too awful, I'd be embarrassed.' But she said these things so he could say 'Women!' with amused exasperation. When she read newspaper articles about women now she got frightened, would retreat, try to build walls of security for herself. It used to work, poetry helped. 'Busy old fool, unruly sun, why dost thou thus, through windows and through curtains call on us?' she'd chant each morning, managing to ignore the fact that Henry was sound asleep and the sun was calling her not away from orgiastic delights but to the washing up and telephoning his agent, which she always did for him. 'You'll miss out on so much,' her mother had said on one of her persuasive days, as opposed to the abusive ones; but right then she had been missing only him, his presence and the sense of space that he gave her; he called her his muse, his holy fire, the priestess of his inner sanctum. Now he was an Anglican who didn't believe in women priests. She wanted to stay there leaning against him, his hands on her neck, because at the end of all, his hands moved her.

'We're going to be late,' he said.

'You can get away with it,' she told him, meaning again a simple fact, but she could sense that he took it as a compliment.

'Funny,' he said as she drove down the road, he peering out of the window as he always did, 'the stereotype of the artist has him completely amoral, and I've never had another woman, only you.'

'Not living up to your image.' And immediately she regretted the bitchiness she could hear in her own voice, because it was gloriously true. 'At his time of life,' her mother had said, 'there's no knowing what he may not have done. You know what artists are, Chrissy, do you really want to be just one more in a long line?' 'No,' she had said, with absolute certainty. 'Only me.' But that had shocked her mother even more. It wasn't till years later that she'd realised that for her mother this was proof in her mother's eyes that he was either a liar or a homosexual and probably both.

'I've abandoned my image,' he persisted. 'Look at me: prosperous, suited, fully employed, living in Rose Tree Cottage.'

'Well, take comfort, you're not a father of four.'

'Thank God.'

She didn't say any more.

She'd forgotten they'd been invited to the Vicarage to meet the new curate. When she entered the room she was surprised to see such a young man there and when she remembered she was even more surprised. New curates have images too and this one didn't fit. He was too physical somehow, too healthy without being beefy and far too beautiful.

'Margaret,' she said to the Vicar's wife, gruffly, because the madonna-like contralto had grown gruff, 'I got in some apple blossom this afternoon. Would you like some?'

Ignore, always ignore the question in people's eyes. She did not look like the wife of a rather famous man, any more than she had, in her neat mother-chosen suits, looked like the wife of a struggling artist. Artists' wives have an image too, and she didn't fit it. Plain solid woman, standing with her back to the fire now, her dress ugly and badly fitting, her legs apart, her face too big for her to carry.

'Chris, how kind.' But the Vicar's wife took kindness as her right; no matter how kind you were you could never measure up to her kindness in letting you try to be kind. What's the matter with me? I like Margaret, she's a friend. She wanted to say, to explain, 'Loveliest of trees the cherry now is hung with bloom along the bough'; tell Margaret how she had gone out this afternoon and seen the crab apple tree almost killing itself in order to have a fragile bloom or two to offer her against her sense of grief and loss. Perhaps she still was a romantic after all.

'I am a great admirer of your husband's work,' said the new curate. There was no answer to that. What could she say? – 'I'm not' or, 'That just proves what a young man you are.' But fortunately he went on, 'He doesn't look at all how I imagined.'

'How strange, that is just what he was saying in the car. But take heart, he does not look like what he is. Now, when I first knew him he looked exactly as you wanted him to look.'

'And you have tamed him?' He said it with a smile, but she still felt a sense of outrage. Her heart cried, No and no and no. He has tamed me. But she smiled and said, 'Are you married?'

'No, I'm only twenty-five and I'm not working yet.'

'When I was your age I'd been married eight years.' And I'd had four abortions and no homes, she wanted to add, but didn't.

'Well,' he said laughing, 'yours was a more romantic generation.'

'I thought it was your age group that had discovered sex and love and the like.'

He looked surprised; for a moment she thought he might be shocked and felt a tinge of annoyance. Well, she could carry off such impropriety on the strength of Henry being a nearly famous artist. But he wasn't shocked. He was surprised. 'You are quite wrong. We are anti-romantics; there is nothing romantic about free love *per se*. Quite the opposite: it is an absence of commitment. Commitment, crazy daft commitment against the odds, and if necessary against the facts, is what romanticism is.'

'Yes, yes, but not commitment to stability. Commitment to yourself, if you like to the gratifications of half-articulated desires. I married Henry when I was seventeen, I gave up "everything" you know from the nice upbringing I had had; he was broke and fifteen years older than me. I was cut off, disowned and to make it all more exciting the forces of the law were all brought to bear to preserve the middle classes' daughters from rape and defilement, so we were taking on a whole social order. That was romantic by any definition. But since then we haven't been very romantic.

78

Quite boringly faithful and true. Faithful and true, my loving comrade.' And part of her knew that she was telling the old story to impress him, so he didn't think of her as a middle-aged dowdy woman.

'But,' he said with obvious pleasure, 'Walt Whitman was a romantic.'

She gave him a grin of delight. She was glad he was coming to live here, she wanted to talk to him, invite him to her house and tell him everything: that her husband called her old thing and took her for granted. That she was fed up with him and his endless demands, with the sameness of her life, with his arrogance and her own impotence against him. That today she had found a perfect crocus and had bent down to touch it and even there in so private, magical a moment he had come wading in demanding that she get ready for a boring evening. She wanted to ask him, 'Was it for this the clay grew tall? O what made fatuous sunbeams toil to break earth's sleep at all?' He looked, she felt that he looked, as though he might know the answers. That she was forty-four and had put on weight, the elegance of her appearance had dropped off somewhere along the line. That twenty-seven years ago she had left her father's house in the middle of the night and taken a train, or rather several trains, to an obscure village in the south-west of Scotland, Newton Stewart it had been called, and had given herself into the care of a wild man with demanding hands; that she had been hungry and overworked and had in the end had five half-formed children ripped out of her gut so that he should not be disturbed; and for what? To drink cheap sherry in a vicarage drawing-room, to be called old thing and to have the dubious pleasure of having everyone she met convinced that it was she who had pulled her husband down from some golden height and shoved him into a suit. She said, 'I'm glad you recognise Whitman.'

And later the conversation shifted to local gossip. The Vicar was worried, one of his most active parishioners was carrying on with a divorcee. 'I can't, I won't countenance a second marriage. I'm not saying I'm not concerned for the poor woman, I'm saying that among my congregation I won't receive a remarried man. I won't communicate him.'

Henry said, 'But, James, everyone is doing it now and anyway why do you want to make sexual sins worse than others? You won't forgive adultery but you will forgive theft, and petty meanness and pride. At least adultery is a sin of love.'

'No it isn't, it's a sin against the sacraments.'

She wanted to generalise the conversation, did not want Henry and James to get dug in theological complexities, knowing they were only teasing each other in any case. She said, 'I can't understand anyone wanting a second marriage anyway. I mean, I can see getting fed up with a husband and leaving, but not doing it all over again.'

'On the once bitten, twice shy theory?' said the curate smiling at her.

'Yes. Yes exactly. I mean, if your experience of marriage was intolerable, why should you want to do it again?'

'But,' he said, 'you might like the state of marriage but not the particular partner.'

'No, no surely that would be impossible. I mean, except for those people who've had lots of marriages or something, your whole idea of marriage is going to be completely integrated with the idea of the person you're married to.'

'Rubbish, Chris,' Henry interrupted her. 'Look at all the women in their late twenties who are desperate for the state of crown matrimonial and don't give a jot who the poor sod is; their ideas about marriage have no relation to the person involved.'

'And the boys.' That was Margaret and she felt a swell of simple pride that whatever she did at least there were some women who wouldn't take it sitting down, 'Look at all the men we know who just want a free domestic, to replace Mummy.'

'Yes yes,' she said, and suddenly it seemed important that they should understand; she felt obscurely perplexed, determined to make herself understood. 'But that's before they are actually married. At some point their expectations and the reality must confront each other and on the facts of that confrontation they'll form their idea of what a marriage is, what it means, and I don't understand how, if they don't like what they see, they'd ever want to do it again.'

She looked round and paused. 'Look,' she said. 'The two are one, the man and the marriage. Henry isn't just Henry to me, he's also my husband. It's not that I know him better or longer than anyone else, I know him differently, in a special sort of relationship. And the state of marriage can't just be the legal condition for me, it's the state of being married to my husband, who is Henry.'

The young man looked at her with warm admiration; she liked that. 'But,' he said, 'you're cheating, you're generalising from your own experience, which, if I may be impertinent, sounds like the mystic union betwixt Christ and his Church. I mean, it sounds like a healthy marriage.' He slowed down, almost embarrassed. She sat there, her large shapeless legs spread out, wide at the knees, her woollen dress stretched out between them, and looked at him. Surprised by joy. I can't even find my own words for my most private experiences. She glowed suddenly, illuminated. The quality of madonna-like serenity reappeared; magically she was a beautiful woman . . . The young man, who alone saw it, realised abruptly why Henry, famous artist, had demanded her. More, he felt a sudden vicious thought of 'lucky bastard'.

In the car going home she wanted to explain to Henry what had happened to her. He was silent. As they got near home he said suddenly, 'Are you looking so beautiful tonight because that young man fancied you or because you fancied him?' But it was not a question, not an accusation, not even a joke; he found her beautiful.

She said, 'Sometimes I hate my fat legs and my ugly hair, sometimes I think they disguise me from the world and I hate them, but I don't change them because they are a part of my flesh. Flesh of my flesh.'

'What are you talking about?'

She turned the car into their driveway and drove into the garage. After she had stopped the engine and switched off the lights, she said to the bright point of his cigarette, 'I love you.' It was not a demand. Not a ritual to summon up the emotion. Like so many of her prosaic gestures, it was a statement of fact.

Much later, when she was almost asleep he said, 'I've just remembered.'

'What?'

'That quotation, "Was it for this the clay grew tall?" 'Member?'

'Yes.'

'It's been on my mind all evening and I've just got it. "Was it for this the clay grew tall? O what made fatuous sunbeams toil to break earth's sleep at all?" It's a poem by Wilfred Owen, *Futility*.'

'Mmmmm.'

'You've known all along, haven't you?'

'Not when I first asked.'

'What made fatuous sunbeams toil to break earth's sleep at all?' He put his hand out on her heavy slightly crepey shoulder and said, 'What a question. The silly sod.'

MISS MANNING'S ANGELIC MOMENT

When she had closed the shop Miss Manning decided on the spur of the moment to go to Mass. She very seldom went during the week, but this was mainly because she kept the shop open late; it made things easier for the wives who worked all day and for the men coming home who wanted cigarettes and things like that, and because she could not bear it when people said that the Asians were harder working than English people. She didn't think she was prejudiced but she also did not want it to be true, so she kept the shop open late even when her ankles felt swollen and tired. They were good friends actually, she and the family who had the nearest small shop to her; they sometimes did her cash-and-carry for her, as her nephew did for them, and they had a clear understanding about milk being for anyone but news-papers and cigarettes for her and sugar and bread for them, even when people sort of made pointed remarks. She tried to take people as she found them, she knew her duty as a Christian. On most days she went upstairs and stayed there, or she went to the Crown, or stopped to chat to anyone who might be around. That was one of the best things about the shop: even though the town had grown and if she went to the centre, which she seldom did, she was worried about getting lost though actually she seldom did – get lost, she meant, though also she seldom went there any more. If you kept a shop people knew you and needed you and you knew them and you knew what was going on, though it was not always best to say what you knew. Her nephew said she ought to retire and she that she could afford to but she had a feeling that there would be little to do except the club and she hated gardening anyway and so she kept putting it off and putting it off, and though she knew the children laughed at her hair and nicked the sweets and that made her sad, she still liked the shop. She liked it, that was all.

So tonight she decided to go to Church. She just decided: there was no special reason but she was not the sort of woman who needed a reason for everything she did and she prepared herself to go. It was not that simple: she did not feel right going in her working overalls – though in her heart she loved the jeans the kids came in on Sundays, she did not herself want to go in her working clothes, on Sundays she always wore a hat, and not many of them did that anymore. If she put a hat on, though, people would guess where she was going and she did not fancy jokes about it the next day. But it was Church, and she had her standards and never mind what the rest of everyone thought about that. In the end she compromised with a woolly beret thing that her great-niece had given her one Christmas, a hat but definitely not a smart hat, and it was cold enough, wintry enough, for that to be unremarkable. She shut the shop, stuck a notice on the door – really she must try and organise a proper closing time and she hoped that no one would think she was ill – and ran upstairs for the beret and her prayer book, smirked at the picture of her father and thought with pleasure and guilt how he would have felt at anyone going to Church, let alone Mass, and never mind calling it Mass into the bargain, on a week day. Then she set off for Church.

She got there rather early. Recently she had started allowing herself extra time to get to places on the grounds that she was slowing down; however, she always allowed herself a little too much extra time so that when she arrived too soon she could tell herself that she was not slowing down all that much for her age. She was old enough to see through her own little plots but they tended to make her laugh at herself rather than be sad or angry. Only tended. She slipped in through the west door and found the Church still in darkness, but the light switches were all the way across the new hall, and she could not be bothered. She knew her way in any case to her own usual pew near the back, and she groped her way there and settled down to her prayers. It was strange to be in the Church in the pitch dark, and to see the bright glowing eye of the sanctuary lamp an unmeasurable distance away, away up by the high altar where God slumbered not nor slept, but she was certainly not frightened. Her papa's children were none of them afraid of the dark, there was no time or place for such nonsense and although she had hated it at the time she had to admit that it did work; well, at least for things like the dark, perhaps not for things like swimming in the deep end, and riding the ferris wheel – she could still remember the sick terror grabbed in his stern arms that had turned all fairs forever into torture chambers for her and how hurt George had been when she would not go with him, no, nearly fifty years ago – and all the other things that she had never dared to do, but she did dare to be in the Church in the dark so that was all right, and the rest better not thought of. She had had a good life any which way. And in any case there was nothing frightening about the Church, she had known it all her life, driven to Sunday School and later finding there something that the rest of her life did not somehow quite provide, and although the dear Vicar had added a whole lot of things when he had first come she had got used to them all by now, goodness what a fuss they had made back then and here he still was and most people now saying that what he did was what they had always done, and there was nothing to be scared of and in a few minutes the dear Vicar would arrive and turn on the lights and light a few candles. She thought even of doing this herself, but remembered that she didn't have any matches and although she could have found the sacristy in the dark and had the key in her bag it hardly seemed worth the effort. She returned to her prayers.

Soon, indeed, the Vicar did come in and light the twin candles far away up at the Lady Altar in the side aisle. She nearly called to him that she was there, but she was right in the middle of a prayer and it did not seem right to interrupt this to chat with the Vicar so she closed her eyes and plunged on.

When, a few moments later, she looked up, she got the shock

of her life. An angel was with the Vicar. The angel was, very properly, wearing a flowing white garment and was holding a branch of candles. And as she watched the angel put the candles down on the choir stalls, went up to the Vicar, placed the angelic arms around him and kissed him, not on the forehead as she had somehow imagined that angels would kiss one, if they were to do anything of the sort, but on the mouth. The Vicar did not seem very surprised, indeed he returned the embrace and the kiss with considerable enthusiasm. Miss Manning, kneeling in the pew at the back of the Church, watched with awe. She had always known, whatever people said, that the dear Vicar was a very good, a very holy man, but even so she had not realised that he was on such very intimate terms with God's holy angels.

Then she had another shock: the angel turned away from the Vicar, so that he was facing her directly and he picked up his branched candles again. His face was thus lit up quite clearly and she saw that it was not in fact an angel but that young man from the polytechnic who was one of the acolytes on Sundays. Miss Manning was, genuinely, a very devout woman; she was also an old one, and in many ways thought of herself as being of the Old School, but none the less she knew a thing or two, and had not muffled herself from the world, as though anyone could who kept a corner shop in an area that she would have to admit had rather come down in the world since her day; but no, although when she had been younger she had not understood all the things that it would have been useful for her to understand she had realised that and later had made an effort. The dear Vicar had once made a very fine sermon on just that, how it was a duty both to God and to natural intelligence to know what was going on in the real world. She had thought that this was quite right and one Lent, about six or seven years ago, she had gone so far as to make a resolution, and had read all the pages, even the business ones, of a good, quality newspaper every day – not that in fact it had proved such a severe penance because there had been a great many interesting things going on and she had rather come to enjoy it which had not really been the point, but only went to show when you came to think about it. However this was neither here nor there, the fact was that she knew what a homosexual was: a man who liked other men instead of women. But it was not something that she had ever really given much thought to, probably better not, although with this AIDS thing that was everywhere it was hard not to wonder a little, though the very idea that God should do that deliberately to anyone seemed to her as bad as getting the disease and she did hope that the dear Vicar . . . but homosexuals, she had an idea that the Bible was not in favour of it at all and that somehow it was not, not something very nice at all; in fact if she had been asked she would have said that it was wrong, and not the sort of thing that people one knew, who went to Church . . . and probably mostly went on in the criminal classes and other poor unfortunates whom it was one's duty to help, and anyway it was not something you had to think about very much and probably much better not to. But this was different, the dear Vicar . . . that sweet young man who was such a Christian, most unusual among those young students, and so polite and kind and coming to Church nearly every day . . . the dear Vicar, such a good man and always visiting and not like the old Vicar in that bullying way. Well, some might not like his High Church ways – she stifled another guilty thought about her father – but everyone said how kind he was, how merry and happy . . . and didn't homosexuals do things in Public Toilets? Well, she would be surprised if the dear Vicar had ever been in one of those in his life, always so clean and his albs and cottas beautifully ironed and so neat always in his cassock, so much better for a clergyman than those open shirts so that one never knew where one was . . . but kissing that young man, what ever was his name for goodness sake? Just like a couple on their way home on Saturday nights and so brazenly, but it was not brazenly because of course they had not known she was there. Miss Manning realised afterwards that if it had been anywhere except the Church she might, she would have been really shocked and angry, but there, in the Church, with the candles, right up by the altar . . . surely the Vicar would never do anything wrong, not really wrong, not right beside the altar, not five minutes before Mass? And they had looked . . . well, they had looked so beautiful, she had thought it was an angel, nothing that was disgusting would make one think of an angel, would it,

87

not ever. Of course there were Satan's wiles, but hardly public, Satan preferred craft and secrecy, she had been taught that, Satan wouldn't risk it with her in the Church and in the middle of 'Soul of Christ'. And it had been one of the most beautiful things she had ever seen, really lovely like, like . . . no, not like a wedding because of all the fuss that people make at weddings and that fanfare and carry-on, more like a baptism, one of those quiet little christenings that some people preferred. Of course she knew what people would say if they knew, there were some people who would say anything, even about the dear Vicar, especially about the dear Vicar, but, she thought, and thought with pride, I don't care. She knew the Vicar was a good man, a really good man and her friend, and just kissing someone, just anything that he might do with the young student who was also a nice person, just that stuff can't make someone a bad man if they are a good person. And it had been very beautiful.

The priest and the acolyte entered and said Mass. Miss Manning said the responses to herself and when the little bell rang she did not go up for communion, she thought it would be better not to. She made a spiritual communion and was sure that that was what God would want her to do. After the service she waited, indeed it would be true to say crouched, in her pew for quite a long time and later crept out quietly and went home without passing the Vicarage, even though it made rather a long detour. She did not care. She felt decidedly happy as she ate her poached egg tea. If it made the dear Vicar happy, if he could do it right there in the Church, up by the altar, so that she thought it was an angel – though of course it was partly her own fault for being lazy about turning on the lights, and even indeed for not going more frequently to week-day Mass despite the Vicar urging them to so often – well, if he could do it and it made him happy, which it must do because he was always so happy and not in that interfering or even frightening way that some people insisted on being happy, then it could not be a bad thing. Indeed it had to be a good thing. And also she had a secret which no one else in the whole town was going to share. Just for once in her life she was not going to be the very last person to hear something. She had her very own secret, and by keeping it she would help the Church and she would help the dear Vicar even though he would never know. She positively grinned at the picture of her father who looked down as sour and disapproving as ever. He's dead, she told herself, and for the first time realised her own glee. Bad luck, she told the picture, you're dead and you can't make me think what you would have thought any more, you silly old man. She did not even quake inwardly. She filled herself two hot-water bottles for a treat and went to bed. As she slipped between the blankets neatly she had a delicious thought: Lent was coming up and Lent meant confession, but this time when she told the Vicar, addressing him as Father, but so different, so wonderfully different, all the private things about herself that no one else would ever know, she would know one thing about him; nothing bad, of course, she would not like that, but none the less a secret thing about him so that he would not be just the representative of Christ, nameless and personless behind the little grill, but real like her, only he would never know.

LULLABY FOR MY DYKE AND HER CAT

꒰ꔛ꒱

The immediate problem is to think of some way to explain it to the boys; for their sake as much as mine – though I can't cope with them peering at me lovingly for the next few weeks and suggesting that perhaps I need a nice rest – which I do of course, but that is another story. And I'm not the sort of person who functions well on Valium, it doesn't suit my style and I think it would be dangerous for the baby. I can hardly use post-natal depression which I thought of at first, because my son is over a year now and having sailed through the whole thing so far I think it would lack credibility. I did consider telling them I had been experimenting with hallucinogenic drugs, but I doubt if they'd believe that either, and the consequences might prove even more complicated than the reality.

Reality is an odd word to use in this context. You see, I thought my son was turning into a cat. Only for a moment or two, and he wasn't anyway, so it doesn't really matter a lot.

When I tell Liz it will make her laugh. At least I hope to God it does. I think it probably will.

I'm not sure if I've ever told you about Liz; she's my best friend. We go back a long way together; as a matter of fact – although this is so corny that we don't often mention it – we met at an anti-Vietnam-War demo in Grosvenor Square in 1968. Neither of us was being particularly heroic, I should say, but we were both with people who knew each other, and then of course it turned out that we were both at college together, so really we had met before though we just hadn't noticed. And if you remember how it was, one thing led to another, and then we were best friends, and before long there was feminism and we discovered that together and fought about it together – both against each other and together against others and we were better friends still. You know people put down the sixties now, it's become trendy to be blasé and dismissive about it, but I go on believing that there was really something there, something important and that those of us who failed to sustain the vision that we had then have something to answer for; and how to know this and hold on to it and still not succumb to the cosiness of Liberal Guilt is a question well worth asking, but one doesn't too often because it is all a bit painful; and we have not been rewarded with the joyfulness and richness that we so optimistically believed in. Or perhaps all I want to say is that those were incredibly happy days for me and I look back on them with nostalgia and regret and the certain knowledge that I blew it and yet totally uncertain as to quite how or when. And a large part of that happiness was having Liz as my best friend and – to be crude – getting the benefit of her extraordinary acute and eccentric mind. And then to everyone's surprise except mine, and possibly Dr Turner's (who was our tutor in our final year and knew damn well that mine was show-off and Liz's was solid) she got an incredibly fancy degree and a research fellowship and I went off to Devon to teach my aphasic children and we did not see each other so much: because she was hardly one to brave the countryside, of which she radically disapproved; and because I was so into hearing those silenced voices and playing with ideas about language and the social construction of the self that I never went away. And then, listening to them so hard, I couldn't take the right line on abortion and we squabbled about that; and she went off to the States for a year and you would have thought that our friendship had come to an end.

But it didn't. I started to write stuff and woke up one morning and realised that, for the moment, the kids didn't have anything more to teach me – I'd never thought that I'd had much to teach them and being them they never made guilt inducing demands for gratitude so I said goodbye and came to London. Then when I was finishing my second book I suddenly realised how much of it I owed to Liz as well as to the children and the school and I put that in the acknowledgements as a good feminist ought and the week *before* it was published the telephone rang and this unforgettable voice said, 'How *dare* you bracket me with brain-damaged infants?'

And I laughed from pure joy. Then she said, 'It's not bad at all and you always did have a way with words but . . .' and with concision and no indulgence she listed thirty-seven real problems with the text. Now it is always flattering to have that degree of attention paid to your work, and also she was enormously knowledgeable – and it wasn't even her subject – but if anyone else I hadn't seen for five years had done that to me I would probably have killed them. As it was, within twenty minutes I had leapt on my bike and was pedalling merrily off to Victoria Park where she was living and where we fell into each other's arms and we were best friends – still or again? I do not know and I do not care.

This is all narrative, it tells nothing, except narrative. And I'm not good at 'the well-rounded character', that stand-by of Western prose literature. I don't know how, within the limits of a short story, to show the way our lives fitted into a much larger web or mesh of friendships and work connections: that is what I want to tell, and also I want to describe her – because I assure you all this does have a lot to do with my present dilemma about explaining to the men I live with how it was that I came to think that my son was turning into a cat. But narrative is not the answer – or not at least to the questions that I want to ask.

Apart from linear narrative there is also anecdote. (There is also analysis, of course, but I think that it is cheating to tell the reader what she has to think about something unless you also tell her the something she is meant to be thinking about: for instance, I can tell you that one of the most delightful things about Liz was that she was extremely witty – faster on her verbal toes than anyone I've ever met, and that at times she would sacri-fice anything, truth, friendship, and innocent people's social comfort, for a good line – but unless I can give you concrete examples of this, which is difficult because all the best jokes come so totally out of context which is long and elaborate and often inaccessible to anyone else, it is not fair on you. You might, like many others, find her humour not charming at all but un-nerving and sadistic and why should you have to take it from me?) Anyway anecdote:

Once she and I were having supper with some people one of whom was a friend of mine who dislikes Liz rather a lot; and the two of us – Liz and I – were showing off rather, and the friend said crossly, bad timing, suddenly heavy, 'For God's sake, you two; stop being each other's *alter egos* and behave yourselves, the way you two go on isn't natural.' Well, I would just have said yeah and let it go at that, but Liz launched into an elaborate though completely accurate description of the reproductive cycle of the *Coriantis*, the Bucket Orchid; and then another about the horsehair worm. (I don't know if you know about either of these natural phenomena, but they both have life-cycle patterns which are so far-fetched, arbitrary and ridiculous that they boggle the mind, make one wonder if Darwin can actually be right, or whether in fact and after all there isn't a delightfully humorous and whimsical old man with a beard up there running the whole show for the amusement of a bunch of angels. You can read about the horsehair worm, if you want, in a wonderful book which practically comes to this conclusion called *Pilgrim at Tinker's Creek* which is written by a woman called Annie Dillard. But I'm getting off the point again.) Liz gave this lecture with great élan and brilliance, if somewhat excessive length. She didn't like this friend any more than the friend liked her. 'Nothing, in nature,' she concluded, 'is remotely natural. Why should our relationship be?'

Once when we were very much younger, I got into a terrible temper and smashed thirty-seven empty milk bottles against the wall of our kitchen. Liz swept up all the broken glass, gave me a hug and never mentioned it again until, over ten years later, when we were talking on the telephone as I described above and she finished her current list of criticisms of my book, she said,

'You see, one for each milk bottle; I've been longing to punish you for that idiotic tantrum.'

Once quite recently we were rather drunk at a large and noisy party; Liz was dancing on the other side of the room and some man – not a very nice one – asked me some question about Liz's early career, and Liz detached herself from the arms of her partner at once and crossed the room and touched his sleeve and said, 'It's not fair to ask Meg those sorts of questions; she's the only woman around who knew me before I was invented.' She went right back to her dancing and I said to the man, 'That's the loveliest compliment I've ever been paid.' And he clearly thought the pair of us were entirely mad.

Once when it was the middle of an extremely cold winter I went round to visit her and, despite several degrees of frost and a howling wind, her cat door was tied open with the lace from her tennis shoes. Shivering I asked her why and she told me that she was afraid that having to push on the icy glass would hurt the cat's nose.

Once. You see, it doesn't work. I've also just remembered that I've forgotten to mention something extremely important about Liz; or rather extremely important to the story that, despite all these digressions, I'm trying to tell you. Well, to be honest, I didn't really forget, I just was not sure at what point to put it in: either in terms of politics, or in terms of artistry. Now of course I've left it so late that it has far more force than I really wanted it to; I feel it to be a fact about her just as the colour of her hair (pale mouse) or her stately bosom and tiny ankles. She's a lesbian. And once, a long time ago, when we were younger, we . . . well, that bit isn't very important. Now I often think that difference helps and sustains our friendship: once we were talking on the phone about whether or not we wanted to go into analysis and she said, 'My problem is when I'm in a room on my own I don't know if I'm alive.' And I said, 'Whereas when I'm in a room on my own I can't understand why I'm not alone.' And this made us laugh with considerable pleasure. I didn't go into analysis as it turned out, but she did: she's quite a lot braver than me in many ways. However, be this as it may, I'm not making very good progress with this story about thinking my son was turning into a cat.

Liz has a cat; her cat is black with a few grey hairs (not dissimilar from mine now I think about it), and quite small and is called Mog. Not directly from Moggie as you might think, but because there are these children's books about a witch called Meg and her cat Mog: they're rather fine books actually and are written in a children's lower-case script rather than proper print. So when I gave Liz a kitten when I first went to Devon and she to Essex and we stopped sharing a flat, she called her Mog because of my name being Meg. People come and go in Liz's domestic life, but Mog stays. She's got old of course and a bit arthritic, and less inclined to frolic; but if you go to Liz's there she will be, as often as not curled around Liz's shoulder and drooped across what we unkindly call 'The Continental Shelf': a wide soft plain created by Liz's breasts.

Liz really loves Mog, in a very simple and pure relationship which I find inexhaustibly touching – a fact which I, like most of her friends, express by mockery and cynicism. When I was first pregnant I went to tell her about it – for some reason I felt extraordinarily nervous about doing so, though I have looked to her and received support in many far less promising ventures – and she looked faintly disgusted. (This did not altogether surprise me, she has the most bizarrely naive views about the facts of life; once when she wanted to find out what heterosexuality was about she asked if she could borrow my cap and was amazed when I told her (a) that this freaked me out and (b) that it wouldn't work.) Then she sighed thoughtfully and said, 'God another damn case of sublimation.' 'What?' I said, startled. 'You know,' she said. 'Another poor heterosexual woman trying to substitute for the fact that she cannot achieve the one perfect relationship in this sad world: the relationship between a dyke and her cat. Haven't you noticed it? Here we all are pushing forty and having to settle for what we can get; and you're all getting babies because you know you can't have what we've got.' Then she collapsed on the sofa in fits of giggles with Mog in her arms. Later she twanged my bra strap rather over-enthusiastically – because I never wore one until I got pregnant when it hurt not to – and said that at least we now had something in common. Later still she bought some beautiful scarlet and black wool and knitted the most wonderful

96

pram suit you have ever seen covered with cabbalistic designs and said if it was a girl would I please keep her in pristine purity until she was sixteen and then hand her over for the traditional *droit de seigneuresse?* After that she did not talk about the pregnancy very much, but the morning that Noah was born she came to visit us both with him still so new that he looked like a tiny interplanetary voyager trying to disguise himself as a human being. And, despite the forbidding notices all over the place, she picked him up and hugged him and said he was nearly as lovely as Mog. But when Paul arrived she swapped bawdy jokes with him about deliveries and knife-crazed surgeons until I felt quite pissed off with the pair of them.

So that is sort of the background; except that I've completely left Paul out of all this somehow. He is the bloke I live with; he and I share a slightly grotty little house with another good friend called David – and it is to them, and now Noah as well of course, that I am referring when I say 'the boys'. I feel a bit overwhelmed to be honest about the number of males there are in my habitation; I had sort of planned on having a daughter to even things out a bit but David and Paul are very old friends and it would be asking a bit much to suggest that David left and there isn't any room for anyone else so there you are. Or rather, there I am, and by and large pretty pleased with it.

So. Last night I had a panicked call from Liz. Mog was sick. Liz was in tears. I have not seen her cry for years; the last time was when I . . . well that would be another long anecdote and I really must get on with this, especially as the anecdotes don't seem to help much. So I chucked the supper-filled Noah at his dad, ignored both their whingeings about it and rode off as fast as I could to Liz's flat, pausing only at an off-licence to buy a large bottle of brandy.

The vet had sent Mog home to die. She had had what seemed to be a twisted gut and the vet had opened her up and discovered that she was riddled with feline cancer. He had suggested putting her down and Liz had refused, refused point blank. The vet had got annoyed with her, said there was nothing more he could do and sent Liz and Mog home. There was nothing we could do either. We sat on Liz's bed with Mog laid out on her Continental

97

Shelf with her eyes slitting up, and we drank the brandy steadily, while Liz petted the dankening fur and I periodically petted Liz. Sometime about two in the morning Mog died. A while later I said as gently as I knew how, 'Liz, she's dead.' And Liz said, 'No, no,' in a little kid's voice. So I took them both in my arms and we just sat there a whole lot longer, and Liz cried and cried and cried, and then she didn't cry any more, she just sat in my arms and held on to Mog. Later still we finished what was left of the brandy, and at about five I said I would have to go because of getting home before Noah woke up and did she want to come? And she said that she didn't, so I said I would take the day off work and come back later with Noah and she said, 'Thank you.'

I admit that bicycling home I realised I was a bit smashed, but not that smashed and it was the darkest night I had been out in for some time and quite windy and spooky, and I'm not a great night person and it is rare to put it mildly that I am out and about at so late and weird an hour. When I arrived the house was silent and dark. I brought the bike in and locked up behind me and went upstairs, suddenly very tired and longing for my bed. At the top of the stairs is Noah's little room; it was more a reflex of tenderness and tiredness that made me go in to look at him than anything else. He sleeps with a night-light on which gives the room a faint and sweet glow. I leaned over the cot as I often do, expecting to be reassured by his sound and total sleep. He was lying as usual on his front with his nappied bottom sticking up in the air and his paw in his mouth, and his whiskers slicked out elegantly; where his sleeper poppers had come undone a little of his soft ginger fur poked out. I thought vaguely that we must get him out of nappies before the summer because it would be too hot for his tail when I realised what was happening. My baby was turning into a cat. And I was so shit scared that I created the most amazing rumpus; screaming and screaming. And Noah woke up and joined in and Paul and David appeared shocked and sleep-hagged, and even in my panic I noticed that David was actually wearing the most preposterous pair of bright yellow silk pyjamas that I had given him for his last birthday and for some reason this did not comfort me. As soon as I had Noah in my arms I realised that it was nothing, nothing at all, a trick of the light, or my tiredness, and he was just my little boy, nearly eighteen months old and only as softly furred as all small human beings are, his face warm and pink and whisker-free. The boys were both concerned and cross. Paul took Noah and settled him down again, and David offered to make some hot chocolate, and I just wanted to be in bed, alone.

You see, I wasn't scared because I thought that Noah was turning into a cat, but because I thought that if he was it meant I was becoming a lesbian and for a tiny moment I felt so relieved. It had been stupid, stupid, and there is no way I can explain it to Paul. I mean it was just a moment of madness, and drunkenness and lateness, wasn't it?

So why am I curled up alone in my bed with some lovely hot chocolate and a unique promise to do Noah's breakfast and crying and crying?

TRIPTYCH

❧

Hagar

In the desert it is hot. It is hot and she is thirsty.

It is hot in the desert and she is thirsty.

The child is thirsty, the child cries, and she cannot bear to see the wasted water as it flows down his cheeks. She licks the tears as they fall and the child laughs, but they are salt and bitter in her mouth. She is too bitter to weep, her tears would scald the flesh, cutting down like the empty gullies of the desert, scald down to the rocks of her bones. She is stripped of flesh and too bitter for tears.

The child is almost too heavy to carry and almost too weak to walk. It is hot. The sun beats and burns on her black hair, because she was too bitter and too proud to accept a head cloth from Sarah's hand. And so she is still, and so she will die. There are things that cannot be changed, not when the desert dogs come out in the desolate cold night and gnaw her bones.

But at sunset, when the child seems feverish and drifts in and out of unkind dreams, and the winds hiss across the sand dunes and the shadows lengthen evil and menacing, then she wonders about pride and bitterness, then she weakens and shakes with fear and longing. But she does not weep.

Before now she has received everything from the hand of Sarah her mistress, from the hand of Sarah her mother, from the hand of Sarah her friend. In the long cold of the night she sets herself to remember; the memories come and go as restless as the child

101

who lies against her shaking and burning through the cold night.

She had been eight years old when Sarah had taken her from Egypt. There had been somewhere before Egypt, somewhere higher, somewhere . . . mother, father, home . . . it is gone and she will never have it back. But it had not mattered because there had been Sarah. Now it mattered because she had to find some place to take the child.

'Little one,' Sarah would laugh in the long trek across the desert, 'little one, you are my immoral earnings. What encouragement is that for a woman to live honestly?' She had still been confused then, only eight years old and brought up in the palaces of the great Pharaoh, a valuable ornament to his court, so black and charming with her fuzzy hair and little pink palms. She had been given to Abraham in exchange for his sister's favours. But Sarah had not been his sister, only pretending, pretending because Abraham was afraid, pretending because Abraham was greedy, pretending because in those far-off days Abraham and Sarah had played a lot, laughing, teasing, joyous. Sarah the beautiful, Sarah the great princess from the noble house of Ur, far far north in the Chaldees. She, Hagar, had never been there, only heard Sarah on long evenings tell stories about the greatest city in the world, about the high walls and flowering gardens, the gold-strewn, ancient city that made Egypt look new and brash and extravagant, the ancient City of Wisdom where it was better to be an astronomer and a magician than a warrior; the oldest city at the very centre of the world where silk and spices flowed in at the east gate and iron and salt and grain flowed in at the west gate and in the centre was the market and the great tower whence the wise could watch the heavens and prophesy not useful but magical things. And there Sarah was a great princess and she had left it all with a laugh to travel God-knows-where with a tough little man whose eyes lit up with a vision and who swore that he had seen in the stars an inheritance for him born like dust out of the desert. And off they had gone trekking the world for fifty years to find that land, that nation, that place they believed they had been promised: that Garden of Eden, that land flowing with milk and honey, that home prepared for them before the flood. And still from her early childhood Hagar could remember, could not forget, the cool loveliness of Sarah, her ready laugh, her carefree calm, and the huge bouncing energy of Abraham, still young, still abounding in hope and merriment and conviction. And they had travelled one year down to Egypt, clear across the desert by the coastal route, because there had been a drought and a shortage in their own land and neither of them saw any cause to go short. And they had pretended that the two of them were brother and sister so that the great lords in Egypt would pay Abraham a bride price for Sarah rather than kill him to marry his wife. The tents on their journey home again rang with merriment at the skill and success of their joke, and she had been a part of the bride price. The little black slave girl who had played on Sarah's couch on golden mornings to amuse the Pharaoh's new mistress.

But . . . Sarah's hands had been warm and gentle. Her eyes laughed but her hands were kind, always, always, till they held out a head covering that she would not take; hard lined hands, old cruel hands, hands that after so many years had betrayed the promise made all those years ago in the land of the Nile. Her hands had been soft and pale then; they had lain on Hagar's naked shoulder as she had whispered to her that she would ask the Pharaoh for her as a gift, and the child had nodded, nodded, nodded, her absurd little braids bobbing with delight, because she had never known kindness before. And Sarah had said that it was good and the child would be safe and would be hers and would be with her always.

Memories of Sarah; Sarah's hands braiding gold threads and complex patterns into her hair. Sarah's arms around her, holding her in the night, in the women's tent, holding her against both their fears. Sarah's hands, strong and commanding, under her own armpits, Sarah's knees, steady and firm either side of her waist. Sarah's breasts soft and warm against her head and shoulders, Sarah's voice gentle and determined: breathe push relax push push breathe breathe down the baby, said Sarah's voice, breathe out the baby strong strong and gentle and steady and Ishmael suddenly rushing down on the strength of her muscles and Sarah's sweet calm. Sarah's hands untiring, loving, washing her with a soft cloth after the labour, washing tenderly

103

and happily, all over, hands like cool honey all over her, mother, friend, lover. Sarah.

She re-calls her memory to her, summoning her spirit back from the cluster of tents, the sheep cropping the sparse hillside grass, the fires glowing and whispering, the night boys moving among the folds with quiet greetings, Sarah's merry laugh, the little comings and goings of an encampment hard beside its well. Back to here, to the cold here of deep desert night, stars huge and distant, uncaringly bright, and the silence so enormous that it stretches for ever, vast and all-embracing. She is thirty years old; she is black as the night itself; she has a feverish three-year-old boy child whose skin is paler than hers, who scarcely looks like her; she is a slave; and she, with the child, is going to die in the desert night and the wind will blow the sand over her bones until it will be as though she had never been. And it will be a loss to no one but herself, she who had thought herself so rich in love.

There has to be a moment of turning, a moment so subtle that one does not notice it, but so perfect that the consequences are inevitable, a moment when everything changes and what is possible before it is impossible afterwards and the unimaginable becomes the normal. Somewhere, at some well side, by some oasis, under some fierce moon, they had all changed: that what had been vision became obsession, that what had been faith became mockery, that what had been love became ownership, and yet still the shadow of what they had been, of what they believed, of their own bright hope and conviction, the shadow of their old selves, hung over those new things unseen, unacknow-ledged, souring what could be a richer and easier joy. Neither of them, not Sarah not Abraham, oh not herself either, could admit, would admit, that they could no longer believe. Sarah became cynical, an edge in the bubbling laughter, an edge turned against herself so that when her child was finally born she called it Isaac – 'God has laughed'. And Abraham had become . . . crazy; receiving ever more bizarre commands from his invisible God, inflicting his ideas upon them with ever more fervour. He had come home once from a half-moon of roaming, staggering into the encampment scarcely able to walk; blood had flowed from under his robe. For a moment Hagar had been carried back to the slave quarters of childhood when the prettiest boys had been made into eunuchs, brutally and publicly; when the loveliest girls had been sent down to the aged crone who lurked, honoured and hated, in the bottom of the gardens of the palace to have their soft inner flesh sliced away with the little bronze knife, so that they might not be tempted to infidelity or desire, and might work out their lives fully attentive to their lord's service, fully complacent to his usage. She had been struck with terror, standing there, the water jar slipping from her hands, slipping and breaking into little sharp sherds while Abraham called all the men of the camp to him – all of them, even her child, and told them that his God had given him a covenant of promise and would winnow the deserts in the night, but would spare the household of Abraham and make his seed like the desert sands. And all they had to do to be worthy, worthy of this great inheritance, was to cut off their foreskins so that his God would know them in that night. Not Ishmael, not her boy child, her joyful bubbling baby then hardly weaned from the breast. Oh let him, Sarah had said, it could be something worse. It could be us. For, years ago, when Hagar had been approaching puberty, Sarah had woken her from recurrent nightmares in which the little bronze knife cut away her tongue, or her breasts or her . . . and Sarah had held her in her arms and promised, promised, promised, that never never never would she let that happen to her and the child Hagar had been comforted. Now she said, it will not hurt, it will not hurt, Abraham would do nothing, never, that would hurt his precious manhood; and she had led Hagar away gently into the depths of the tent and covered her with a blanket and kissed her ears and eyes and mouth and genitals so that she would not have to hear the screams of her mutilated child. And as so often, Sarah was right, and within hours Ishmael was bumbling and buzzing again, but why had Sarah not spoken, why had Sarah kept silent in the tent, smothering Hagar with kisses rather than challenging the madness that grew in Abraham, rather than telling him that there was no God that would seek to damage the children of the promise? Was that the moment when they had changed? When they had given up, when they had realised that Abraham would if he thought fit sacrifice his own flesh and blood to please his deranged and unreasonable God who grew, with each passing year, more and more like Abraham himself.

Or was it when Sarah started returning from his tent not laughing and full breasted, but irritable and sore? When her monthly blood-letting ceased and her skin wrinkled not just along the lines of her smile, but sagging away from her cheeks and lying in dead folds around her neck. Her husband's desire was no longer toward her, but only toward an ever more desperate pumping of his seed into her barren sack, more demanding, more cantankerous, more fanatical as her hope faded and her beauty dimmed. She who had left Ur for him, whose wisdom and beauty and calm steadiness had kept them safe for half a century of adventuring. And he turned his lust towards her own maidservant, her child and her friend. No, she had said, no. And Hagar, steadied by Sarah's firmness, had said no, too; though actually there was something about his eagerness and his conviction. Then, after too long and when any possible pleasure had gone out of it, Sarah had changed her mind; oh do it, Hagar, for God's sake. Get the old goat off both our backs. We need a child in the tents, an end to sheep girls' mockery of me, an end to this obsession. Let him give us some peace. The two of them had lain together in the women's tent and Sarah had urged her, urged her, urged her to consent to him. She had said and said that it was Sarah that she loved, Sarah that she served, that she whored for no married men, and Sarah in a sudden fury told her that she was the mistress, that Hagar was hers, hers to do as she willed with, and if she chose to use her to get children for her old age then that was just Hagar's bad luck. From the day she had received into her own hands Hagar's seal of ownership Sarah had never, ever, not once, mentioned the relationship between them until that night. Hagar had pushed Sarah away from her, stood up, stripped naked and in front of Sarah had oiled her body, flaunting the long full curves of her buttocks and thighs, asked Sarah with impudence how her husband liked it best, how he would respond to virgin flesh, tight and sweet, after years of aged flesh, and with her mouth tasting of vomit she had gone out into the night and did not return for six days; and when she returned it was with a haughty knowledge and a wide sneer.

They had made up, delighted in the pregnancy, together in the birth, they had fondled and loved and embraced, but something had changed; had changed because Sarah who had called her daughter, called her beloved, called her friend, had now also called her slave and used that power over her; had changed because she let Sarah do so, because she had acted on Sarah's commanding against her own heart, because she had, named and hurt, accepted the naming, she had acted like a slave. She would never do so again. But they had together set the scene for their own betrayal of each other. And the roads of a woman's life lead clearly, straightly forwards; the seed that is sown will be the grain that is reaped, and in choices made in anger, made in pain, made in loss, the future is forged more certainly than the smith at her fire can temper the iron.

They were happy for two years, happy in their child. Hagar and Sarah's boy-child made both his mothers happy. Hagar tries, with the child dying in her arms, to hold on to that sweetness, but it is not enough. She who had no mother and no lover has lost her mother and her lover, and in the darkness of the night she knows that she will lose the child too.

But they had not chosen, and could not have chosen, and by then would not have chosen, either of them, Sarah's pregnancy. It was Abraham's victory and he strutted it before the whole encampment while Sarah was sick, stomach sick and heart sick for nine long months, embittered, sour, cross, frightened and ill. Hagar knew that, knew those things, but could not move out to her, could not understand, would not understand. When Sarah's child was due Hagar took her son and ran away into the desert; she knew the love with which Sarah had held her through that dark country in which a woman must travel searching for her child and bringing it back strong and well. Sarah had been, on that hard journey, her strength and her stay, but she could not give it back again. She could not and she did not know why she could not. It was not seemly that flesh so old should be fruitful; it was not seemly that the woman who had held her so lovingly in her arms should hold another child there. For ten days she had roamed, and it should have been a foretaste but was not, because that which is chosen, that which can be re-chosen, is different, is totally different from that which is forced upon one. She had been oddly happy those ten days away from the encampment, away from Sarah's bitterness and Abraham's obsession – the two of them had marked her life, marked it with joy and grief, but marked it beyond the reasonable; they were neither her parents nor not-her-parents; they had both been her lovers, the parents of her children. Her household, both chosen and given. For ten days she had been a free woman. Then she had gone back. Sarah was trying to suckle an obdurate, large-nosed, cheerless baby; a night screamer and day whiner, a fretful unsettled baby, not like her golden boy. 'What's his name?' she had asked. 'Isaac, that is "God laughed",' said Sarah, without laughter.

And the rest was perhaps inevitable. She, Hagar, could not bend the neck that Sarah had taught her to hold so stiff. She, Sarah, could not bend the neck that Hagar had allowed her to hold so high. Isaac grew, Ishmael grew, in stature and in love of their mothers. But his birth, too late, and in an unexpected moment, did not allay Abraham's fears. Isaac was not reared in the women's tents but in the courts of the men. She and Sarah found it hard to talk, to meet, to kiss, to be together.

There was a long week when she did not see Sarah, when Sarah was in Abraham's tent. Once she heard Sarah cry, cry out in pain and in loss, but she did not go there, they were the courts of the masters and if Sarah chose to be there that was her matter, not Hagar's. She would not ask for entrance, knowing that it would be forbidden to her. And where now were all the brave promises, the bright and childhood faith in the covenant, in the invisible and unknowable Lord who held all people in equality, for which they had gone out from their lands, from their known places, from their certainties?

'Sarah feels that it is not right that the son of Abraham should play with the seed of slaves,' said Abraham.

'He is the son of Abraham,' she muttered. But when he said he could not hear her she did not repeat it, she did not dare.

'Sarah says that you set yourself up against her in a manner unbecoming to a slave girl,' said Abraham, and now Hagar did not know what they were saying. Abraham in that week they had been together had venerated the purple blackness of her breasts, had been amazed and delighted by the different colours flowing over her body: plum, indigo, black, crimson, pink, scarlet, nut, ash, honey, ochre, cream. The rainbow sign, he said as he stroked her, and she had believed him. The rainbow sign, the sign of hope and promise. The old lecher.

'Sarah has asked me to have you leave the camp.'

She looked at Sarah once, and Sarah first lowered her eyes and then raised them and in them was a mute appeal, so beaten, so defeated, so unbearable, that she did not look again.

'You want her to go, don't you, Sarah?'

There was a silence. Both of them had pleaded for her. Surely she had the power. Even now, even in the great darkness of the desert, to believe that she could not have defied him was more painful, was even more painful than to believe that she could have and did not.

The silence stretched. Every man in the encampment, every man who had known how they loved each other and had not liked it, every woman who had known and who had seen it as a sign of hope, had waited.

Wielding his power, the power they had all given him, freely and in love, over fifty years, he said, 'Don't you, Sarah?' And Hagar could feel the force of his will, the depth of his desire and need that Sarah should say it.

The desert wind hushed to hear her answer, it seemed in that encampment that the sheep themselves, the sheep the final arbitrators of their being, the lining and basis of their wealth, of their survival, paused to hear that whisper in the air: paused to hear Sarah say, 'Yes.'

And Hagar could not afford to see the black bruises round Sarah's eyes and neck; because dear God, she would rather, she would rather die here in the desert than acknowledge that Sarah could not have said otherwise.

Abraham, satisfied, took the child and set it on her shoulder and gave her a water skin, filled, and a sack of bread ready baked, both of which she accepted, and she turned from the camp and set out upon her lonely journey, and when Sarah came to her and offered her a head cloth, against the sun, against the sun of the desert, she had looked at her with dignity and said, 'If my son were to starve before the first well I would not accept any gift from your hand. You took me as nothing out of your charity and you can dispose of me as nothing. I am yours to command.'

She saw the tears spring in Sarah's eyes, and Sarah's tears sprang from deeper in her than any woman she had ever known, but tears were salt and would not comfort her child or her soul when the sun beat down on them. Sarah had chosen. Understanding was pointless, was too expensive, was unafford-able, when you were the black slave girl and she was the wife. In bitterness she said, 'I am yours to command.' It was the only insult available to her after so many years of love.

And now she was in the desert and pride was a bitter fruit, born from an evil root, and she wished she had been a woman who could beg and plead, and she was not; and she was not because Sarah had been her mother. There, there, was the pain; there was the unbearable, unsustainable truth. That Sarah, who had taken her from the land of the Pharaoh and told her she was lovable, who had touched her black skin and found it lovely, found in it the source and power of resistance and had given back to Hagar that strength which she had drawn from her, that it was Sarah, that it was love, which had betrayed her, which had given her child over to the desert dogs to maul in the darkness. That the name of Sarah, the name of love, that was the taste of tears, of bitterness and of thirst in her mouth, the tears that made her child smile even as he choked on them.

The dawn comes, the sun leaping up garish and sudden, no moment of grace between intense cold dark and blinding hot light. And with the morning comes despair. So she takes her child and lays him in what little shade she can find, under a scrubby tenacious bush, clinging against all odds to life in that bright wilderness. He is weaker now, bleating occasionally like an animal, and fretfully curling and uncurling his fingers. She knows he is dying and she cannot bear it, so she crawls away, moaning, and sits down about a bow-shot's distance where she cannot hear his whimpers, where she will not see the moment of his death. She cannot watch him die. She seeks no shade for herself but sits cross-legged, upright, and the sun rises over her head. And by mid-morning she is half-crazed with grief and heat, and still she sits not looking at her child, looking instead straight into the sunlight which crashes against her eyes. The only black thing in that burning gold space.

And then, the world flickers . . . the whole world quivers . . . the world turns, shifts, the stars crash against each other . . . and then the world moves deep under her and the sun stands still . . . stands over her head. And then . . . and then . . . tongues cannot tell nor words proclaim what things have been prepared for those whom God loves. There is a shadow, a great cool shadow, and at the heart of the shadow is perfect darkness, blackness so thick and soft, as black and soft as her mother's breast in her high homeland of Cush, and she can taste the sweetness of the milk from those black breasts, which are like Sarah's breasts, and in the heart of the blackness are black flames which purge, burn, reduce all things to black ash, to the purity of darkness and beauty. And the great black God caresses her, arms as strong as kind as Sarah's arms, arms as fierce and tender as her mother's arms a thousand miles a thousand years ago in the mountain place where all people are black. To be touched by so much beauty where she has not been used to see any is aweful to her and she tries to cover her eyes, but she would not accept a head cloth from Sarah's hand so she has nothing to cover her face with. And God takes her by the chin and raises her head and says, 'Look, look, look at me.' And God says to her, soft, loud; wrapped within the God she hears Her speak and She says, 'What troubles you, Hagar? Do not be afraid for God has heard the voice of your silence. Get up and give the child a drink of water, for I will make you mother of many nations.' And God strips her of her clothes and caresses her, kisses her sweeter than dreaming, and the great black smile of God makes her laugh a laugh as merry and dark as Sarah's laugh once was. And God grins delightedly and is gone.

And here is Hagar, dancing, dancing naked on the desert dancing floor, leaping and singing and laughing, the long curves of her body absorbing the bright sunlight and turning it into the

111

darkness of God, refracting, consuming, kaleidoscoping blackness, a new thing born of a brave moment. And Hagar leaping sees, sees that no distance away there is a spring, a spring of black water, sweet and wholesome, and she fetches the child a drink, and takes him by the hand and leads him over to the spring and together they built a sand heap, knowing and laughing that the wind will blow it away almost before they have completed it, but it is an altar in their own honour, and Hagar smiles and says, 'Here, here I will mark the place because here I have surely seen Her who sees me. I have seen God and lived.'

And they travel safely. Although it is hot and thirsty in the desert, they travel safely, south and west, until they come to the shores of the Red Sea, and there, not bothering to ask God to part the waters for them, they take passage of an Arabian dhow and so come at last to the beaches of Hagar's homeland. And she is full of joy.

Sarah

In the tent it is cool. It is cool but she is sweating.

It is cool in the tent but she is sweating.

For years I have heard Sarah's voice; for years I have strained my ears to hear it, identified with it. Not just I think the sharing of names, though that should not be discounted. It is easy for a woman like me to hear the voice of a woman like her; two women, of different time, place, space, race, but two women of privilege, articulate, sophisticated, adept, self-controlled. Women, even, of power, by class, education, marriage, status. I hear her voice too easily, Hagar's too furtively. But now . . . it is cool in the tent but she is sweating.

She is sweating with shame and confusion. Sarah is blushing – a deep hot flush that she thought she had finished with ages ago. She is blushing, sweating, ashamed. For herself. She does not like it.

For no matter how I context it, Sarah's laugh in the tent, by the oaks of Mamre, rings uncomfortably in the ear. Sarah the beautiful whom kings have desired. Sarah the courageous who followed her adventurous husband throughout the whole world. Sarah the charming, who has created and sustained a loving and fruitful relationship of great complexity and delicacy for so long. Sarah the gracious, laughing in the tent curtain and trying to deny it so that her husband's guests will not be embarrassed. Sarah the old and barren.

Why is she laughing? What are the echoes and the vibrations of her laughter? That uncomfortable, stifled laughter will not quench Hagar's thirst in the hot desert. She is laughing because it is too late. To be pregnant now will be a final twist of fate by a God who has ignored her for too long. Once, she used to pray to Him, begging Him for the child who would cement her crazy husband to her, and later praying for the child to fill the gap that seems enormous to her now that she knows that she cannot love the man she left her lovely homeplace for. Once she prayed with the same zeal and faith as he does still. Then she learned that this

113

God of his was not hers. Everything she knew of now belonged to Abraham: the sheep, the servants, the tents, herself. And his God, too. That it is not so somewhere else, far away, in the scented courts of her childhood, is little or no comfort to her. She left them proudly, she cannot return. Abraham's God does not listen to a word she says to Him. After a while she stopped believing that her prayers would be answered; after a little longer she stopped praying.

Hagar, however, is young and lovely. Sarah despises Abraham for fancying her. She is lovely, but she is neither wise nor beautiful as Sarah was. The Pharaoh of Egypt has desired Sarah, to this she holds when there is little else to hold to. But, none the less, Hagar is lovely, and young. Sarah loves her: she loves Sarah. Neither of them love Abraham who pesters Hagar with his hot, but old, hands. With a slave's sensitivity to what is and is not permissible Hagar tells Sarah that Abraham fancies her; she does not tell Sarah that the old man disgusts her. With a wife's sensitivity Sarah knows this anyway and decides it will be best for all concerned if she ignores it.

Sarah is a woman of great dignity. She is not prepared to have her husband touching up slave girls behind the tents. She is not going to have Hagar, her maidservant and friend, made a byword for sheep boys. She loves Hagar: the energy that she once directed towards her husband is now redirected. Some evening when Hagar is brushing her hair, tenderly back away from her face, brushing it admiringly up from the nape of Sarah's still glorious neck, sending shivers of pleasure down Sarah's spine, Sarah reaches up a single hand and touches the younger woman's wrist, or she leans back so that her head rests on the pliant stomach of her friend. Hagar is young enough to be her daughter; she has won this lovely daughter for herself. She decides she will let it be easy, and from then on it is easy. She lures the two of them to bed, teasing and encouraging Hagar, binding Abraham more subtly to her will. Hagar's baby is therefore her baby; she created the relationship that conceived him. Ishmael is her delight, her son: she had achieved him by the use of all the power and skill that she holds in her own two hands.

'Ishmael, Ishmael,' she calls, and he comes, crawling, staggering, then running, from Hagar to Sarah and back again. Sarah is not jealous, at this time, of Hagar. She and Hagar are good friends. They share the child, they share the relief, never quite named, that Abraham, now satisfied in his obsession, bothers them both less. They feel free to concentrate on their son. Sarah is, for now, perfectly happy; for now she is a mother twice over. A mother to Hagar whose man she chose with truly maternal care, whose back she supported through the long night while the child was pushed laboriously towards life, that great and mighty work, that costly and rewarding labour. A mother to Ishmael, because she called him into being, not by lust but by intelligence. Moreover she no longer has to endure the embraces of that senile goat whom she used to love, and for whom she sold her own life and thought it a bargain.

She stifles her laugh in the curtains of the tent, because it is not a very nice laugh. She does not now want Abraham's child: she already has her own children. This is a last trick by Abraham's God. Although she does not believe that Abraham's God listens to her or cares about her, she has no doubt at all that He exists, and that her husband and his God plot together to get the best of all possible worlds for Abraham.

She thought she had outwitted them and now her puny body is going to betray her.

There is no more faith possible.

'Why are you laughing?' Abraham and his God's messenger say.

'Laughing? Me? I wasn't laughing.'

'You were laughing. Don't you believe that you are going to have my son? Don't you believe that my God can do anything He wants to?'

Her laughter turns to racking sobs, but the men do not hear them. The sobs continue painful, unending, for nine months. Isaac is born. Her body is too old for this and it takes its toll. She hates Isaac. He is not her son, because she did not consent to him. Instead she consents to her own degradation. She lets Abraham make her say it, she lets Hagar be sent away. Isaac looks like his father from birth. He is not beautiful and spoiled like Ishmael; he is sturdy and clever and arrogant. She weeps and weeps. Hagar and Ishmael are sent away. She is defeated and she punishes the only person she can punish. Abraham wants Hagar out, and Sarah consents. Punishing Hagar she is punishing herself, and she feels Hagar's hatred and is, for a brief moment, glad of it. She cannot talk to anyone; nor can she forgive herself. Hagar and Ishmael have to go; they must not be allowed to confuse the issue, to detract from Abraham's real son. As the mother of his son he loves Sarah again, and she hates him for that too. Abraham hears her anguish; he says that Sarah is jealous of Hagar and Ishmael, and that this will spoil her milk. Ishmael sucked at her empty breasts for the simple pleasure of it, but Isaac will not feed from her at all. Her breasts are huge, swollen, revolting, but her son will not feed from her at all. The milk will not flow, her tears flow instead. She wishes she were dead and that will not help. She does not want Isaac, she wants the children of her heart and mind, not this child of her gut, so she condemns them to die of thirst in the desert. She knows that she will not ever be forgiven.

When she hears the messenger speak, down by the oaks of Mamre, she knows that she, who has plotted and schemed so carefully for so long, has been outwitted. The joke, subtle and tortuous, is – like all the best jokes – a matter of timing. She is a sophisticated woman. Of course she laughs.

She laughs at herself and all her plotting. It is best to laugh at foolish women who think they can get their own way in a world where even God is a man and on the other side.

Abraham

I thought, I really did, in all sincerity, that I would write Abraham's story too. I thought I would write it here, like the others, trying to recreate it, enter in to it, understand it; tell it.

But I'm not going to.

Not because I think I couldn't do it. On good days I have immense faith in the power of my own imagination (and other people's too of course). If I want to do that sort of story I can, and will. I even have now and again, though not often. (Whether men can do women's stories is another question, one that feminist literary discourse asks often; but it is certain that the oppressed develop insights about their oppressors to a greater degree than the other way about because they need them in order to survive – a sort of natural selection, like Darwinian evolution.) So, no, it is not because I don't think I could not do Abraham's story, but because I can't be bothered.

Anyway, almost everyone knows it already. If you really don't, and you really want to, here's what you should do. Sneak into almost any second-rate hotel (there are hotels both too grand and too grotty for this to work, but a decent old-fashioned railway hotel, for instance, will do nicely, and so will one of those vast international chains where every branch looks identical, like a Holiday Inn). Open the drawers of the bedside cabinets, and in one of them you will find – sometimes accompanied by adverts for local car-hire firms etc. – a fairly bulky hard-covered book. This is entitled *The Holy Bible* and has been placed there by a charitable organisation which holds Abraham's version of this story dearer to its heart than I hold it to mine. This *Holy Bible* is not a single coherent text and should not be read as such. It is rather a curious, and very beautiful anthology – poems, stories, philosophy, helpful maxims, ethics, diet advice and mythology all jumbled up, a sort of *Commonplace Book of Western Culture* (no I haven't forgotten the Greeks) put together by a slightly crazed editor. Never mind all this: the first – and from a reader's point of view one of the best – section of this anthology is called

117

Genesis, which is itself an anthology. Chapters 12 to 25 deal with Abraham's story. Chapters 16, 17, part of 18 and 21 deal particularly with his relationships, if such they may be called, with Hagar and Sarah.

(The rest of 18 and 19 will introduce you to a nasty little tale of homophobia and misogyny. Don't miss it. Ask yourself rather how it fits in here.)

So now you know Abraham's story; the story of the first patriarch. I could not have told it better myself. So instead of telling it again I am going to put on my theological hat and give you a few brief notes from the *S.L. Maitland Biblical Commentary*.

i) From a literary aesthetic point of view the whole thing is chaotic, clumsily narrated, muddled and repetitious. Incidents, clearly garnered from different sources, are confused, conflated, reused but not integrated. This reflects the extraordinary skill of the compilers: only by lulling the reader half asleep with tedium and confusion can they hope to slip past her some intolerable sets of attitudes, some moral turpitude of such depth that normal concepts of ethics cannot even address the material and at the same time manage to persuade 3,000-years-worth of readers from diverse cultures, philosophies and social contexts that is the wellspring of God's will towards justice, of decency, of normality.

ii) Father Abraham is, frankly, a real bastard. Among other things, he lives off his wife's immoral earnings (cf. Chapter 12 verses 10 – 20 *et al*); he is prepared to bump off his supposedly beloved son in order to please his boss and gain material advantages (Chapter 22). He is almost certainly insane and demonstrably selfish, autocratic, lecherous, cowardly, violent and megalomaniacal. All these things are renamed 'virtue'. This is called patriarchy.

iii) Here we see, perhaps for the first time in recorded history, one of the classic devices used by men against women. Sarah, the wife, gets blamed but not punished. Hagar, the mistress, gets punished but not blamed. Abraham gets neither; he has his cake and eats it too. This is neat.

iv) The compilers, despite what has to be seen as a first-class job, make two very serious errors. Firstly, in the face of their best efforts, they dismally fail to write out, or suppress, the abiding emotional reality of Sarah and Hagar. At their every appearance the text vibrates, leaping, shining, buoyant, alive. It is there, it is undeniably there – Hagar praising in the wilderness, Sarah laughing in her tent. Their vitality searing the pages across the long silences.

Secondly, and even more seriously, the compilers failed to edit out an extraordinarily and revealing fact. There is only one person in the *whole* of this weird and wonderful book who 'Sees God and Lives'. And she is Hagar, slave, foreigner, unmarried mother; the woman expelled from the protection of the encampment, driven out of the book, the woman who sojourns in the desert, the outcast, the stranger. And there she is, singing, dancing, rejoicing. How can we not rejoice with her? Whatever were they thinking of, those priestly, juridical editors, that they let her dance undamaged in the mid-day sun?

You probably don't like the tone of this bit of the story. I don't blame you, I don't really like it much myself – edgy, cranky, cynical; it is not even 'proper fiction'. Let us get back to the mythic, the lyrically imaginative, as quickly as possible. Let us bring that hyped-up prose, that imaginative understanding, that poetic psychoanalysis, to bear on that poor crazed old man; let us explore, illuminate, perhaps even beautify those dark corners of his driving obsession.

I do wish I could. But it is too soon and too late. To understand all is to forgive all. And I do not want to forgive. I cannot forgive. I am Hagar who is driven into the desert. I am Sarah who betrays her friend. This nasty cynicism which destroys joy, hope, transformation, magic, truth, love, it is still necessary, still – as always – a useful mutation, an adaptation vital to the survival of the species. As we dance, dance on the hot sands and rejoice, as we laugh, laugh in the cool tents and weep, we must remember and give thanks for that too, alas.

FLOWER GARDEN

—————————— ✿ ——————————

Elsa Schiaparelli as a small child 'planted seeds in her throat, mouth and ears, in the hopes of transforming her ugly duckling self into a beautiful flower garden'.

Observer, 24 November 1985

Yes indeed. It makes so much sense of what came later, that elegance of artifice pushed beyond all sense into a new realm of adornment, that amazing *trompe-l'oeil* knitware, those hats the shape of shoes.

Because of course the seeds would not grow there, would they? Even if their tiny determinations escaped the huge hands of mammas and nannies, ferreting them out and flushing them away, still they would not grow in so cold and barren an environment – ear wax and nasal mucus do not provide the dark damp secrecy that germination requires.

But.

But the desperateness of the infant female knows no bounds. Which of us did not desire it, that magical transformation into the desirable?

The beginning of my story is easy enough.

Ageratum, Alyssum and Alyssum saxatile, Anchusa Blue Angel, Antirrhinum. Aquilegia (Columbine), Aster, Aubretia, Begonia.

She had not anticipated the range of choices. She is too old, she realises almost sadly, to be taken in by the profusion of colour in the pictures; her father is a keen gardener, he is standing further inside the shop discussing bonemeal with his friend the shop keeper, it will take him hours, but when he is finished he will want to leave immediately. From years of watching him at work she knows how great the difference between the illustration and the reality is – art wins over nature all along the line although she has not yet formulated the words for this. Also as a gardener's child she knows enough to know that the circumstances matter, the soil and the sunlight and the seeding ground. Begonias, for instance, will not do, they have tuber roots – she needs some simple hardy annuals, bright and glittery in colour, fast-growing, summer-flowering, shallow-rooted. The brooms are beautiful and her father loves them dearly, his tiny garden has several: their long slender branches bearing a profusion of small flowers, bizarrely elaborate in their colouring; but they will not do any more than the Begonias – they take years to grow and they have rough scratchy branches. She has seen her father bring home small broom plants, their balled roots wrapped in strips of dustbin bag. But she passes by the ornamental cabbages without a qualm, they are definitely not what she has in mind; the same applies to the cacti, only more so, she almost giggles.

Calendula, Campanula, Candytuft, Canterbury Bell, Carnation, Chrysanthemum

The Chrysanthemums distract her from her business, reminding her of school too much and of those words that are difficult to spell: she is irritated, the names of the flowers were pleasing in themselves and now she thinks with anger of her elder brother who can spell everything and on whose shoulder her father's hand rests gently when he comes in from work. She is twelve years old and terribly, terribly unhappy. She hates her new school. All that passionate intensity that only a far distant year ago she put into her friends and her games and the life of her secret imagination is now directly purely and miserably towards her school, where she is lonely and wretched and stupid. She has tried to tell her parents and they do not listen, or they listen but apparently do not hear. They said, 'You'll get used to it,' and when she didn't they said, 'Come on lovey,' and, 'You only get out what you put in.' They told her it was a very good school, which seemed entirely irrelevant to her, and that very nice girls went there, which seemed ignorant and untrue, and how the hell

122

did they think they knew? Now they were getting angry with her; they said things like, 'Pull yourself together,' and, 'Do you call that mess homework?' and, 'Don't slouch,' 'Don't scowl,' 'Don't shout,' 'Don't go on and on about it.' And, 'If you want to make yourself that ugly, go upstairs and do it in the privacy of your own room; don't inflict it on the rest of the world.'

She could not find words to tell them, to explain to them about the enormousness of the building and its ugliness; the vast barren acres of wall that scared her and muddled her and she was never on time, and how there was no time allotted for transit. How she was meant to be in one place at one moment and another immediately after but they were miles away and none of the other kids liked her, and her friend had been sent off to boarding school and why couldn't she go too? And the dread, the stomach-churning dread, of the bus ride in the morning when the huge boys from the senior school teased her and her brother sat and watched them with a smirk on his face and refused to be on her side. And she did not understand what they were saying but it was horrible.

And now. She used often to come with her father to the garden centre, and had wandered about the nurseries and asked him about different plants and sometimes he even let her choose something, or would buy her packets of seed or ask her if she thought some new variety was pretty and she had thought that he did it because he wanted to be with her and because he liked her and would help her, but this morning coming down to breakfast she had heard him say to her mother, 'All right then, if I have to I'll take her, I know you deserve a break, but honestly.' She writhes now in misery and shame, wrapping her arms round her body and caressing her own ribs through the pink sweatshirt which her mother had bought for her last year. Then she'd said, 'Isn't it funny, darling, this is probably the last time I'll be buying you children's clothes. It makes me feel old.' But the shirt still fitted; it didn't really it was too short in the sleeves but it still, well, fitted in the sense that her mother meant. Her body was like a wooden log. There was something wrong with it. It was ugly. Ugly. Ugly.

But the names of the flowers were not. Beautiful, soothing, a

123

magic spell. She returned to them, blotting it all out briefly, incanting down the list, inspecting each packet on the flimsy metal stand with determination.

Cockscomb, Convolvulus, Cornflower, Dahlia, Daisy, Delphinium. Euphorbia, which she called Snow on the Mountain. Felicia, Freesia, Gazania, Geranium, Globe Amaranth, Godetia, Gypsophila – Baby's Breath.

The names are magic, distant dreams of beauty and sweetness and safety. Her parents called her Rose, because she had blossomed pink and sweet on a golden summer morning, they had told her that over and over again. They had been going to call her Helen after her grandmother but when they had seen how lovely she was they wanted to name her after a flower. She had liked that story and now she did not believe a word of it.

'Rosie,' called her father from up the shop where in the half dark he and the shop man were mixing together foul-smelling substances which would make the lawn grow sweet and green, 'Rosie, I'm going out with Jack to look at some new fuchsia he's got in. Do you want to come?' He was lovely, her father, his moustache lay along his lip looking silky, but it wasn't it was rough and scratchy; when she had been tiny she had played a game with him when he would try and scratch her cheek while she snuggled in his lap attempting to crawl her head up the inside of his jumper. He was very good looking, she thought, and turned to go with him, remembering good times in the back yard with him and Jack, where the other customers weren't meant to go and had to wait outside and be helped by 'the girl' who knew nothing about plants and could never work out the price of half a tray. Then she remembered that he didn't want her, that he had not wanted to bring her, that he was probably embarrassed to be seen with her now she had turned out so hideous. 'No,' she said, 'I'm busy.' And saw not a look of loss but a flicker of irritation. 'OK then, don't get up to mischief.'

Of course she would have to steal the seeds to make it work. She hadn't realised that until now. It had to be wicked. She was wicked and bad and ugly. She was a witch with secret powers. Now was her opportunity. But her nerve failed. She could not decide what she wanted.

124

Something poisonous and evil – Foxgloves full of dangerous drugs, Laburnum whose pods could kill you, Yew berries plucked from church yards at dead of night, Deadly Nightshade – she would like to grow deadly nightshade, like the witches in *Macbeth*. If there were butterfly-attracting plants, were there toad- and bat-attracting plants, too? That was what she wanted. She would teach them. She would grow Deadly Nightshade in that very secret garden and mix the red berries in her parents' drinks and that would teach them. Or perhaps it would poison her, the long heads of Foxglove, Digitalis, make her heart pound and beat until it split her open and then they would be sorry. That would teach them a lesson: they thought she was ugly and stupid and dull and sulky, but she had power. Her mother knew and was afraid of it.

'Rosie, if you want to play on that swing, I think you should wear trousers.' Her father noticed too but he never said anything. Just the other day she had come downstairs with no knickers on and sat on the floor with her legs crossed, and he had noticed and he had not said anything. He had looked. Yes, he had looked. But not because of the power. Because, because her skin there was not like her mother's, foxy-furred, lush. Actually she looked like a badly plucked chicken, white and sickly. In the evil-smelling flower garden, though, she would grow her flowers and they would blossom forth wild with delight. Dark and damp, seeds at least liked that, and she would be a garden. But she had to choose. It was her secret.

Hollyhock, Jacaranda, Larkspur, Lavender (too sweet and old ladyish for her schemes), Linaria, Lobelia. Love-lies-bleeding.

Damn. No. That she did not want, cascading out of her. The roots of the flowers might stop it, that blood, she did not want that, ever, ever.

Lupins, which were hideous, her father would not have them in his garden, Marigolds, Mecanopsis – the beautiful blue poppies that she anticipated finding in heaven in the old days when she had believed in heaven, Myosotis (forget-me-not), Nasturtium, Nicotiana, promisingly wicked that and smelling so sweetly. Pansies were babyish and Passion flowers not what they sounded, nothing to do with that but with Jesus and stupid old church.

125

Phlox, Pink, Polyanthus, Primrose, Primula – like they had taken her mother when she went in the hospital just after she had begun at the horrid school and no one would tell her why, she was not having them inside her. Rudbeckia, Salvia, Scabious, Silene, Smilax, Stock.

She is beginning to panic. She must make her selection before her father comes back. If he sees her buy seeds he will want to help her plant them, he will be pleased with her and see her as co-operative and good, but she is planning something more powerful and strong than he can dream of. She will surprise him with her beauty and her sweetness, but she must do it, he must not help her, she does not want him to know, to help, to offer. No one must know. She has to crouch down now, she is getting near to the bottom of the seed display frame. If she cannot decide soon she will have to move on to the vegetables. That will not do.

Sunflower and Sweet Pea.

More varieties than she can cope with and they will have to be staked. She could not bear to drive in a stake right into her heart like a vampire. She wants no one's blood, not even her own. It is not blood she is seeking.

Sweet Sultan, Sweet William.

But he is not and only God knows how much she hates him, and that is why she does not believe in God any more – he smirks in the bus when the other boys make remarks. Why has he not told her parents, why have they not noticed that she has to go all that way and be the only girl until they arrive in Brook Street and then Stephanie gets on whose breasts are there and whose hair is in fat copper-coloured curls and the boys still make remarks, but different, kindly, admiring, they do not run their hands down her back to laugh because she does not wear a bra, they do not pinch and flick at Stephanie who is beautiful and clever and lovely and sixteen. She loathes Stephanie and she wants to be like her, be her. She smiles, Stephanie does, at the boys, but she never smiles at her; sometimes she encourages them to mock at her they say hateful things, about how ugly and skimpy and unlovable she is and William sits there and smirks. Now she is hurrying, missing packets, and yet still unable to stop until she reaches the end.

Tagetes, Thunbergia, Verbena, Veronica, Viola, Viscara, Wallflower, Zinnia.

There is a Zinnia called Envy and it is Chartreuse green. Her hand reaches out towards the packet, to grow green flowers, the flowers of the forest and the envy of the gardeners. She hears her father and Jack coming into the back of the shop and straightens up. Now she cannot reach the Zinnia and she is glad. Envy is not what she wants. In seconds it has all gone wrong. She wanted only to be beautiful, to be beautiful and beloved. She reaches out almost vaguely and takes the packet nearest to hand; she shoves it up front of her pink shirt and turns towards her father. She has never stolen anything in her life before. Her shirt feels transparent, both the seed packet and her flat button nipples tingle under his and Jack's eyes. She will not care. She summons a soft smile. When he sees her father's eyes crinkle with pleasure she knows how good a smile it was. Side by side they leave the shop together.

All day she smiles and is charming. She expresses a keen interest in the bonemeal fertiliser her father has purchased. She helps her mother in the kitchen, washing up with a rather sweet but willing ineptitude. She tells them a funny story about her history teacher at the school. She participates in a conversation about their summer holiday, even when William comes in and contradicts everything she has said. Her parents are relieved and then delighted. They have not had such an agreeable Saturday for months. They respond easily to her good will, they build on it, apparently lovingly. By early evening she has almost deceived herself as well as them, almost desires that it should be this way, that they have been right and all she has to do is make an effort. But upstairs in the drawer, tucked away under her hair ribbons, the little packet is waiting for her. She knows it is there and that her parents are foolish to be so easily deluded. They think she is their sweet little rose, growing in their tidy garden, a little bonemeal will keep her blooming; they do not know that she is jungle and desert, dangerous and wild. She is too ugly to live in the lovely and orderly garden that her father has made for her. She is too important and powerful to be pruned into his shapes. She senses her own confusion dimly, and senses it as excitement.

127

It is bedtime and she kisses them nicely and goes to her lair. She opens the drawer carefully and for the first time examines the packet.

She has chosen Candytuft (*Iberis*), Dwarf Fairy Mixed:

Easy to grow, colourful border plants producing pretty little clustered heads of flowers in summer. Regular in height, brilliant range of shades. Ht. approx 15 cm. Sow March – July where intended to bloom.

It couldn't be better. The hands of the gods were guiding her. She almost giggled to think that she might have snatched up some ornamental thistle.

She takes off all her clothes and stands in front of the mirror. Her body is flat shapeless bony. All the things the boys say on the bus. Ugly. Above the scrawny shoulders – 'Darling, do drink your milk, you're too thin' – her hair hangs straight and straw-like. Her face is plain; her eyebrows too heavy, her skin yellowy and blotchy, her mouth too big, her nose too small. Ugly. She looks like a deranged chicken. Her tummy sticks out and she has no other curves. Her legs run straight down, skinny and shapeless. Ugly. Ugly. Ugly. She forces herself to look at her crotch, white and pallid, plucked chicken waiting for the oven. Ugly. Slowly she takes the seed packet and folds it so that only the picture shows; then she holds it up against her crotch and smiles. She will be exotic, lovely, lovable. She will be weird and wonderful, mysterious, powerful. She will be sexy. Her father will love her. He will come with her on the bus and shut the boys up. He will shout at William and wipe that smirk off his face. He will tell her mother . . . her fantasy fails her suddenly. She removes the packet and turns away from the mirror. She cannot quite decide what she wants her father to say to her mother. Time will tell, she thinks, mimicking her mother's own mimicry of the cliché.

Now she is decisive: she opens her bedroom door and listens; from below she can hear the television. She will be safe. She skips still naked along the corridor and into her parents' bedroom; she rummages through her mother's things with swift graceful hands, thorough but disturbing nothing. Briefly she considers a life career as a burglar. She extracts one of her mother's tampons from the box and then after a pause a second one. She wants to take the instruction sheet too but fears that her mother might miss it: surely it could not be that difficult to put in? Perhaps there was some use in those horrendous 'personal hygiene' classes the school laid on for them. From the bathroom she collects a toothmug and fills it with water.

It turns out to be lucky that she had taken the two tampons. Her first idea had been to soak it in water before sprinkling the seeds on it, but when she extracts it from its wrapping and tube and puts it in the toothmug it fans out, rather beautiful but, she feels certain, uninsertable. Its limpness in her hand suddenly disgusts her and she breaks out of her room to flush it down the toilet.

But the seeds will need watering, will need dampness in order to sprout. She knows that. She knows too a way, her need making conscious something she has done all her childhood but without awareness. She does a new thing therefore when she lies down on the bed, face downwards, the packet of seeds beside her, and places her three middle fingers on her pubic bone, curling the tips inwards. So great is her sense of adventure and obsession that the whole thing works with extraordinary ease, not the soft bedtime comforter, replacing thumb and teddy unnoticed years ago, but power and will, and a belly deep mounting confidence in herself and her authority. She reaches with her spare hand for the packet of seeds and lays it flat against her stomach: it is its stiff cold shape against her own flesh that makes her come and she feels both sacred and scared.

And after that it is quite simple to lick her finger and dip it into the seed packet and then wipe the seeds off as far up her vagina as she can reach; it takes a number of finger loads before she is satisfied that there is enough. Then she takes the tampon and inserts that too, tamping it down carefully as her father would tamp down the earth over his planted seeds. She reminds herself that in the morning she must remove the seed packet and the tampon tube and throw them away at school on Monday; she thinks that after about ten days she will remove the tampon and the seeds should have germinated. She does not think any further than that because she falls asleep satisfied.

✻　　✻　　✻

I said that the beginning of the story was easy – relatively easy, at any rate. It is the end of my story that is hard, because I do not know what would happen next and no one seems able to tell me. Would seeds germinate in an adolescent vagina? Yeast grows well there, as too many of us know to our discomfort, but Candytuft seeds? In primary school biology I learned that germination requires darkness and wetness and warmth; certainly those conditions are fulfilled. But pH levels, the relative acidity of vaginal secretions versus plain water, the changes and fluctuations of conditions?

I do not think that even if they germinated the conditions would be suitable for full flowering, do you? 'The only way to find out', said my friend Jill after we had worked our way through two evenings of speculation, 'is to try it.' It was her idea about the tampon incidentally, both as a moisture preserver and as a rooting substance – like the cotton wool she and I and doubtless many other children used to grow mustard and cress. But I cannot bring myself to do so. I do want to know the answer, for Rose, for myself and for what has become pure curiosity, but I cannot actually do the experiment. I consider it and am alarmed at the spectre of infection, or at the very boldness and weirdness of wanting to know. Nor can I now, because it is too late, just guess and tell the story that way – not because it would be dishonest since this is after all a fiction, but because I would not be satisfied, emotionally. So I have written two endings.

1. Rose is still a little child. She cannot bring herself to wait the full ten days, in fact she cannot bring herself to wait even twenty-four hours. On Sunday evening she pulls out the tampon to see what is happening, even though the more mature part of her mind knows that nothing will have happened yet. Although she reinserts it some of the seeds have fallen out and she does not know accurately how many are left. She repeats this on Monday and Tuesday, nicking another tampon from her mother's drawer since the first one is getting somewhat grungy and increasingly difficult to reinsert. The discomfort and fidgetiness of all this is taking away from the sense of excitement and power that she had when she started. She also remembers the great delight of

masturbation and further disrupts the potential germination process by exploring this now more interesting process. On Wednesday there is a new girl on the bus when she goes to school. Because she is new and the boys have as it happens something more interesting to talk about they ignore the two little girls who sit near the front and smile shyly at each other. When Stephanie gets on the bus the new girl leans over and whispers, boldly, but as it turns out she is a bold child, 'Cor, get 'er, is she the school tart?' Rose and she then giggle all the way to school and all the way home again in the afternoon. By Thursday they are best friends. Now that she has a friend and no longer has to face the misery of the journey or the scariness of the long bleak passageways, Rose begins to enjoy herself. On Friday morning she extracts the tampon finally, notices that none of the seeds show the least signs of germinating and has a reasonably good try in the bath at washing herself out. She abandons the project, embarrassed to think she could have been so loony, turns her attention to the business of growing up in the real world, finds that her parents are not actually sadists, but decent well-meaning people who are, like all parents, a bit thick but still OK more or less. They had also been right in their handling of the whole situation, it had been 'just a phase' their daughter had been going through. Rose lives happily ever after, or at least until she gets a desperate crush on her biology teacher.

2. Rose is a very stubborn adolescent who is deeply and truly unhappy. The sense of power and self-determination that the adventures of Saturday gave her are extraordinarily important to her; the whole experience has the quality of obsession. Despite the mounting discomfort, she does in fact rigorously and disciplinedly keep the tampon in for ten days. By this time she has a stomach ache, a constant violent itching and a discharge, which is yellowish, curdy, foul smelling and ugly, ugly, ugly. On the tenth day she extracts the tampon and finds that the seeds have indeed germinated, but, instead of beautiful green shoots, her vagina is full of what look like rock worms, colourless, translucent wriggles. Her disgust at her body mounts, it is hateful, ugly and incapable of producing anything of worth. She throws up violently and flushes

her vomit and her experiment down the loo. However, the discharge, the itching and the stomach cramps do not diminish. Her mother, doing the family laundry, eventually notices the discharge and tries to speak to Rose about it. Her daughter however is in such a misery of pain and guilt that she sulks, withdraws further and refuses even to speak to her mother. The mother, not entirely unreasonably, panics now, notices how unwell her daughter is looking and jumps to parental conclusions. She drags Rose off to the family doctor, an action which, in her anxiety, she manages to present as a punishment rather than an attempt to get help. The elderly and not unkindly meaning doctor manages to extract from Rose what has happened but with so little tact and usable sympathy that far from feeling better she feels worse. The doctor also feels duty-bound to tell the mother. She freaks out. The father when he is told is so totally embarrassed and unable to cope that he loses his temper and yells at Rose, who is now not only suffering from severe pelvic inflammation but from suicidal impulses as well. Her brother, whose problems I do not have time to go into now, thus becomes privy to his sister's secret, and one evening in a long misogynistic and beer-laden rap session with his friend tells the story as a further proof of the utter weirdness, disgustingness and dangerousness of women. Within a week all the senior school boys know and within ten days so do all the girls. Within two weeks Rose, from remarks made on the bus, knows that they all know. She lives unhappily ever after, or at least until she finds a women's group where in sisterly solidarity she learns that she is not a total freak.

But there is another ending. A dream ending, as sweet and tender as so lovely and adventurous a young woman deserves.

3. The flowers grow; uncurling inside her, in an environment so perfectly safe and delightful that they sprout faster and stronger than usual. Rose tends to them lovingly; the weather is bright and sunny and she creeps off into the high hay field behind the house each afternoon after school and naked spreads her legs for the sun to bless her fruitfulness. The shoots grow green and leafy, tiny buds form on them and they spread themselves out exquisite and charming

around her pubis. She takes great care of them, delicately trimming and pinching out the lead shoot to keep their firm bushy shape and taking great care not to crush them. Admittedly this means that she has to forge her mother's signature to get her out of school games for a whole month, but a little self-interested lying is not necessarily bad for a young woman growing up. Now she has something more interesting and precious to think about, she does not mind the taunts of the boys on the bus, and can secretly gloat over their ignorance and uncreativeness. At last the young plants flower, in all the promised shades of white and cream and pink and purple. They are beautiful. She is quite enchanted with her own body and with her own power. She is beautiful. With some skill she lures her father up to her bedroom; as she hears his footsteps on the stairs she whips off all her clothes and spreads herself out for him. He opens the door and stands there looking at her for a whole long minute, then he says, 'Darling, how beautiful, how clever of you, you must have worked so hard.' He grins affectionately and says, 'Quick, quick, we must show Mummy, she'll be so proud.' And he calls for his wife and she comes and stands beside him and looks too and says, 'O my love, what a beautiful surprise.' And holding hands they walk across the room to inspect her flowering body more closely.

'Wow,' says the mother, 'I could never have kept such a secret; you are clever.' 'They're beautiful,' says the father, 'and you're beautiful.' And without letting go of his wife's hand he leans down without touching her body and picks just one head of the flowering Candytuft and his wife pins it in his button hole. Then he grins at her cheerfully and says, 'I'll tell you what, pop on a loose frock so they don't get squashed and we'll go and show Nan and Gramps.' So later that evening, with their woman child in the middle, the three of them go hand in hand dancing down the road to visit her grandmother and show her the beautiful flowers.

A FALL FROM GRACE

❧

Those years the children – in Brittany, Bordeaux and the Loire Valley, even as far away as the Low Countries, Andalusia and the Riviera – missed their acrobats. In the Circus the dingy wild animals, the clowns, illusionists and freaks remained, but earth-bound. Gravity held the Circus, and the mud, the stench and the poverty were more evident. The magic-makers, the sequinned stars that flashed and poised and flew and sparkled through the smoke above the watchers' heads, the death-defiers who snatched the Circus from the mud and turned it into flowers and frissons, were gone.

Gone away to the strange camp on the Champs de Mars, where they were needed to help Monsieur E. build his beautiful tower. Oh, the local residents might tremble in their beds with fear at the fall from heaven; intellectuals and artists might protest that 'Paris is defaced by this erection'. But the Circus people, the artists of body and philosophers of balance (with wild libidinous laughs at so unfortunate and accurate a turn of phrase), they understood; the acrobats – without words and with a regular fifty centimes an hour – knew. They alone could comprehend the vision. They knew in the marrow of their bones and the tissue of their muscles the precise tension – that seven million threaded rods, and two and a half million bolts could, of course, hold fifteen thousand steel girders in perfect balance. With sinews and nerves and cartilage they did it nightly: that tension and harmony

135

against gravity was their stock-in-trade. Their great delight was that Monsieur E., a gentleman, a scientist, knew it too, and knew that they knew and needed them to translate his vision. High above Paris they swooped and caracoled, rejoicing in the delicacy and power of that thrust, upwards, away from the pull of the ground. And so they left their Circuses, sucked towards Paris by a dream that grew real under their authority – and for two years the acrobats and trapeze artists and highwire dancers and trampolinists abandoned their musical illusions to participate in historical, scientific reality.

Eva and Louise too came to Paris. Not that they were allowed to mount up ever higher on the winches, hanging beside the cauldrons which heated the bolts white hot; not that they were permitted to balance on the great girders, shifting their weight so accurately to swing the heavy strands of lace into place. Their skill, as it happens, was not in doubt, but they were women. They drifted northwards, almost unthinkingly, with their comrades and colleagues, simply because the power of Monsieur E.'s vision was magnetic and all the acrobats were drawn inwards by it and Eva and Louise were acrobats. And they lived with the other acrobats on the Champs de Mars, poised between aspiration and reality, and the city of Paris went to their heads and they were, after a few months, no longer who they had been when they came.

Their Circus had been a disciplined nursery for such children. Born to it, they had known its rhythms, its seductions and its truths from the beginning. Precious to their parents because identical twins are good showbusiness, they were only precious inasmuch as they worked and made a show. With each lurching move of the travelling caravans they had had to re-create the magic from the mud. Only after the hours of sweat and struggle with the tent, with the law, with the unplanned irregularities of topography, and with costumes which had become muddy or damp or creased or torn – only then were they able to ascend the snaking ladders and present the New Creation, where fear and relief were held in perfect tension; where the immutable laws of nature – gravity and pendula arches, weight, matter and velocity – were apparently defied but in fact bound, utilised, respected and controlled; where hours of dreary practice, and learning the capacities and limits of self and other, where the disciplines of technique and melodrama and precision were liberated suddenly and briefly into glamour and panache. And still were only a complete part of a delicately balanced and complete whole which included the marionette man, the clowns, the seedy lions and the audience itself.

But Paris, and a Paris in which they could not do what they were trained to do, was a holiday, a field day, where the rewards were quick and detached from the labour. As the tower grew so did Eva and Louise, but the tower was anchored and they were free-floating. They learned to cross the laughing river and seek out the *boîtes* of Montmartre. Here, their white knickers and petticoats frothed easily in the hot water now available to them, they learned to dance the new dance – the Cancan. Here their muscularity, their training, their athleticism stood them in good stead. They were a hit: with the management who paid them to come and show off round bosoms, shapely legs, pink cheeks and bleached petticoats; with the clientele whose oohs and ahhs were more directly appreciative than those of any Circus audience.

Yes, the beauty and the energy of them as they danced and pranced and watched the tower grow and watched their comrades labour upwards. They walked under the spreading legs of the tower and laughed at the jokes called down to them; they ran among the tents and teased the labourers; they turned the odd trick here and there for affection and amusement, although they could get better paid across the river where the rich men lived, Monsieur E., coming each day to see how his dream was developing, soon learned their names and would stop and smile for them, and they smiled back, arms entwined with each other, but eyes open for everything that was going on in the world. And they reassured him of his beauty, his virility, his potency, all of which he was manifesting in his tower which broke the rules of nature by the authority of science and the power of men. One day he told them, for the simple pleasure of saying it, for he knew they were simple girls and simply would not understand, that when his tower was finished it would weigh less than the column of air that contained it. The girls laughed and wanted to know why then it would not fly away, and he laughed too, indulgently, and explained, paternally, about displacement. But from then on the idea of the tower simply, ooh-la-la, flying away with them was fixed in Eva and Louise's minds and it made them laugh because of course they knew that it was impossible.

And walking in the streets and parks they learned new styles of dressing and new styles of living; and their eyes were wide and bright with delight. Having little to do all day they wandered here and there, through boulevards and over bridges. In the flower markets they were overcome by the banks of sweetness, the brilliance of colours; in the antique-shop windows they saw the bright treasures from China and Egypt, from far away and long ago; and in the cafés they smelled new smells and heard raffish conversations about things they had not even dreamed of. And everywhere they went, because they looked so alike and smiled so merrily and were always together, people came to recognise them and smile at them, and they felt loved and powerful and free as they had never felt before. All Paris was their friend and the city itself was their Paradise.

They were a hit too in the *Salons des Femmes*, where the strange rich women, who dressed like men and caressed Eva and Louise like men too, were delighted by their health and energy and innocence. And by their professional willingness to show off. Louise enjoyed these evenings when they drank tiny glasses of jewel-coloured drinks and performed – dances, tumbles, stage acrobatics – and were petted and sent home in carriages. But Eva felt nervous and alarmed; and also drawn, excited, elated and it was not just the coloured concoctions that made her giggle all the way back to the Champs de Mars and swear that they would not go again. In the dark warmth of the bed they shared, Eva's arms would wind round Louise as they had done every night since they were conceived, but her fingers crackled with new electricity and she wondered and wanted and did not want to know what she wanted.

And of course they did go again, because it was Paris and the Spanish chestnut flowers stood out white on the streets like candles and the air was full of the scent of them, giddy, dusty, lazy. At night the city was sparkling and golden and high above it the stars prickled, silver and witty. And Monsieur E.'s tower, taut and poised was being raised up to join the two together. In the hot perfumed houses they were treated as servants, as artists and as puppy dogs, all together, and it confused them, turned their heads and enchanted them. One evening, watching them, the Contessa della Colubria said to her hostess, 'Well, Celeste, I think they won't last long, those two. They'll become tawdry and quite spoiled. But they are very charming.' 'I don't know,' Celeste said, 'they are protected. By their work of course, but not that; it must be primal innocence to love, to be one with another person from the beginning, with no desires, no consciousness.' 'Innocence? Do you think so? Perhaps it is the primal sin, to want to stay a child, to want to stay inside the first embrace, the first cell.' The Contessa's eyes glittered like her emeralds. 'Do you think it might be interesting to find out?' Celeste turned away from her slightly, watching Eva and Louise across the salon; she said quickly, 'Ah, *ma mie*, leave them be. They are altogether too young for you to bother with.' The Contessa laughed, 'But, Celeste, you know how beguiled I am by innocence. It attracts me.'

She was mysterious, the Contessa della Colubria, strange and fascinating; not beautiful *mais très chic*, clever, witty, and fabulously wealthy. She had travelled, apparently everywhere, but now lived alone in Paris, leaving her husband in his harsh high castle in Tuscany and challenging the bourgeois gossips with her extravagance, her outré appearance and the musky sensation of decadence. Rumour followed her like a shadow, and like a shadow had no clear substance. It was known that she collected the new paintings, and Egyptian curios and Chinese statues; it is said that she also collected books which respectable people would not sully their homes with, that she paid fabulous sums to actresses for ritual performances, that she slid along the side of the pit of the unacceptable with a grace that was uncanny. But she had created a social space for herself in which the fear, the feeling, that she was not nice, not quite safe, became unimportant.

She took Eva and Louise home in her carriage that night. Sitting between them, her arms around each neck, her legs stretched out, her long narrow feet braced against the floor, her thin face bland, only her elongated ophidian eyes moving. The sharp jewel she wore on her right hand cut into Louise's neck, but she did not dare to say anything. The Contessa told them stories.

'You see the stars,' she said, and they were bright above the river as the carriage crossed over it. 'Long ago, long long ago, it was thought that each star was a soul, the soul of a beautiful girl, too lovely to die, too bright to be put away in the dark for ever. The wild gods of those times did not think that so much beauty should be wasted, you see. Look at that star up there, that is Cassiopeia, she was a queen and so lovely that she boasted she was more beautiful than the Nerides, the sea-nymphs, and they in their coral caves were so jealous and angry that they made Neptune their father punish her. But the other gods were able to rescue her and throw her up to heaven and make her safe and bright.

'And those stars there, those are Ariadne's crown; it was given to her by Bacchus who was the god of wine and passion, not an orderly god, not a good god at all, but fierce and beautiful. Ariadne loved Theseus first, who was a handsome young man, and she rescued him from a terrible monster called the Minotaur who lived in a dark maze and ate people. Ariadne gave her lover a thread so he could find his way out and a sword so he could kill the monster. But he wasn't very grateful, as men so seldom are, and he left her on an island called Naxos.'

'I know those ones,' said Louise, pointing, breaking the soft flow of the Contessa's voice with an effort, 'those ones up there, those are the Seven Sisters who preferred to be together.'

'The Pleiades, yes, how clever you are. And you see that one of them is dimmer than the others. That is Meriope, and her star is faint because she married, she married a mortal, but the rest are bright and shiny.'

Louise's neck hurt from the Contessa's sharp ring. She felt tired and uneasy. She wanted to sit with Eva, their arms around each other, tight and safe. She did not understand the Contessa. But Eva liked the stories, liked the arm of the Contessa resting warm against her skin, admired the sparkling of emeralds and eyes and was lulled, comfortable and snug, in the smooth carriage.

The balance shifted. They knew about this. As Eva leaned outwards and away, away from the centre, then Louise had to move lower, heavier, tighter, to keep the balance. As Louise pulled inward, downward, Eva had to stretch up and away to keep the balance. On the tightrope they knew this; but it was a new thing for them. There was another way, of course; their parents had had an act based on imbalance, based on difference, based on his heavy grounding and her light flying, the meeting-place of the weighty and the floating. But they had not learned it. Even in the gravity-free place where they had first learned to dance together, in the months before they were born, it had been turning in balance, in precise sameness. It was the poise of symmetry that they knew about; the tension of balance. And it was foolhardy always to change an act without a safety net and with no rehearsals. They did not know how to discuss it. The difference was painful, a tightening, a loss of relaxation, of safety. The acrobat who was afraid of falling would fall. They knew that. But also the acrobat who could not believe in the fall would fall. They knew that too.

The Contessa took them to a smart pâtisserie on the Champs-Elysées. She bought them frothing hot chocolate, and they drank it with glee, small moustaches of creamy foam forming on their pink upper lips. They were laughing and happy. 'Which of you is the older,' she asked, 'which was born first?' 'We don't know,' said Eva and giggled. 'No one knows. We tumbled out together and the woman who was supposed to be with my mother was drunk and she got muddled up and no one knows.' 'If they did it would not matter,' said Louise. 'Our mother says we were born to the trade, we dived out with elegance.' Eva and Louise were pleased with themselves today, with the distinction of their birth, with their own inseparability, with the sweetness of the chocolate and the lightness of the little apricot tartlets. The smart folk walked by on the pavement outside, but they were inside and as pretty as any grand lady. And in the bright spring sunlight the Contessa was not strange and dangerous, she was beautiful and glamorous, she was like something from a fairy story who had come into their lives and would grant them wishes and tell them stories.

The Contessa came in her new toy, her automobile, roaring and dangerous, to seek them out on the Champs de Mars. She was driven up in her bright new chariot, and stopped right between the legs of the tower. The acrobats swarming up and down, labouring, sweating and efficient, swung aside to make space for her, as she uncoiled herself from the seat and walked among them. And she knew Monsieur E. and gave him a kiss and congratulated him on his amazing edifice. Louise did not like to see her there, but she invited them into her car and they rode off to the admiring whistles of their friends. 'In Russia,' the Contessa told them, 'the people ride in sleighs across the snow and the wolves howl at them, but it does not matter because they are snugly wrapped in great furs and the horses pull them through the dark, because it is dark all winter in Russia, and the motion of the sleigh is smooth and the furs are warm and they fall asleep while the horses run and the night is full of vast silences and strange noises so that they hang bells on the horses' bridles, and all the nobility speak in French, so that people will know how civilised they are, and not mistake them for the bearded warriors who live in snow houses beyond the northern stars. And even the women of these people wear high leather boots and ride with the men on short-legged, fierce horses. They ride so well up in that strange land that ordinary people have come to believe that they and their horses are one: they call them Centaurs, horses with human heads and trunks and arms. Long, long ago there were real Centaurs who roamed in Anatolia and knew strange things and would sometimes take little babies and train them in their ways and they would grow up wise and strong and fit to be rulers, because the Centaurs taught them magic, but for ordinary people the Centaurs were very dangerous because they were neither people nor animals, but monsters.'

And they rode in the Contessa's car around the Bois and she took them back to her house and taught them how to sniff up a white powder through slender silver straws and then they could see green-striped tigers prowling across the Contessa's garden with eyes like stars, and butterflies ten feet across with huge velvet

142

legs that fluttered down from the trees like falling flowers. And when they went home they found they could believe that Monsieur E.'s tower could fly, and they could fly on it, away away to a warm southern place, but they did not want to leave Paris, so they waved to the tower and they were laughed at for being drunk, and they did not tell anyone about the white powder.

One day at a party, in a new beautiful strange house where they had been invited to do a little show, the Contessa sought out Eva for one brief moment when she was alone and said, 'I have a pretty present for you.' 'Yes, madame,' 'See it is earrings.' She held out her long, thin, dry hand, the palm flat and open, and there was a pair of earrings, two perfect little gold apples. 'These are golden apples from the garden of the Hesperides; Juno, the queen of all the Gods, gave them to Jupiter, the king of all the Gods, for a wedding present. They grow in a magical garden beyond the edge of the world and they are guarded by the four beautiful daughters of Atlas who carries the world on his back. And around the tree they grow on lies a huge horrible dragon who never sleeps. So you see they are very precious.' Eva looked at them, amused; she had little interest in their value, but liked their prettiness. 'One for me and one for Louise, madame?' she asked. 'No, both are for you. But you will have to come by yourself one evening to my house and collect them.' 'But madame, we always go together, you know that.' 'Eva,' smiled the Contessa, 'I'll tell you a little story: once there was a woman and she was expecting a baby, and she wished and wished good things for her baby and especially that it would grow up to have good manners. Well, her pregnancy went on and on, and on and on, and still the baby was not born. And none of the wise doctors could make any sense of it. And in the end, ever more pregnant, after many many years, as a very ancient lady she died of old age. So the doctors who were of course very curious opened her up and they found two little ladies, quite more than middle-aged, sitting beside the birth door saying with perfect good manners, "After you," and, "No, no, my dear, after *you*". C'est très gentil, but what a waste, what a waste, don't you think?' Eva giggled at the silly story, covering her mouth with her hand like a child.

She did not care about the earrings but she knew that if she went to the Contessa she would find out, she would find out what it was she did not know, what it was that made her nervous and elated. She could feel too the weight of Louise, the weight of Louise inward on both of them, the weight swinging out of balance. She had to correct that inward weight with an outward one. Had to remake the balance, the inward weight with an outward one. Also she wanted to know, and if she went she would know that and something else perhaps.

'Yes, madame,' she said, 'yes, I will come.'

And the Contessa smiled.

She did not know how to tell Louise. She could not find any words for what and why; they have never needed words before, they have not rehearsed any. Next Tuesday she would go to visit the Contessa. This week she had to find words to tell Louise. Instead she drank. Louise, who knew she was excited but could not feel why, could not understand, could not pull Eva back to her, drank too. Their comrades on the Champs de Mars thought it was funny to see the girls drunk; they plied them with brandy and wine. Drunk, Eva and Louise showed off, they performed new tricks, leaping higher, tumbling, prancing; they do not stumble or trip, they cannot stumble or trip. They are beautiful and skilful. This is their place. The men clap for them, urging them on. In the space under the tower they dance and frolic. They start to climb, swinging upwards; from each other's hands they ascend. Somersaulting, delighting, they follow the upward thrust of the tower; its tension, its balance is theirs. The voices of the men fade below. Once, as they rise above seven hundred feet, they falter. 'It's your fault,' says Eva, 'you lean in too hard.' 'No,' says Louise, 'it is you, you are too far out.' But they find their rhythm again, trusting the rhythm of the tower that Monsieur E. and their hard-worked colleagues below have structured for them. On the other side of the river they can see Paris, spread out for them now, the islands in the Seine floating on the dark water, the gay streets shining with golden lights. Above, the sky is clear: the moon a bright dying fingernail, the constellations whizzing in their glory. The tower seems to sway, sensitive to their need. It is not quite finished, but as they approach the top they are higher than they have ever been, they are climbing and swinging and swooping upwards. Suddenly both together they call out to one another, 'It was my fault, I'm sorry.' The rhythm is flowing now, their wrists linked, trusting, knowing, perfect. It is their best performance ever. Down below the men still watch, although it is too dark to see. They know they will never see another show like this. They know these two are stars. They make no error. They do not fall. They fly free, suddenly, holding hands, falling stars, a moment of unity and glory.

But it is three hundred yards to the ground and afterwards no one is able to sort out which was which or how they could be separated.

THE WICKED
STEPMOTHER'S LAMENT

※

The wife of a rich man fell sick and, as she felt that her end
was drawing near, she called her only daughter to her bedside
and said, 'Dear child, be good and pious, and then the good
God will always protect you, and I will look down from heaven
and be near you.' Thereupon she closed her eyes and
departed. Every day the maiden went out to her mother's grave
and wept, and she remained pious and good. When winter
came the snow spread a white sheet over the grave and by the
time the spring sun had drawn it off again the man had taken
another wife . . .

Now began a bad time for the poor step-child . . . They
took her pretty clothes away, put an old grey bedgown on her
and gave her wooden shoes . . . She had to do hard work from
morning to night, get up before daybreak, carry water, light
fires, cook and wash . . . In the evening when she had worked
until she was weary she had no bed to go to but had to sleep by
the hearth in the cinders. And as on that account she always
looked dusty and dirty, they called her Cinderella.

You know the rest I expect. Almost everyone does.

I'm not exactly looking for self-justification. There's this thing
going on at the moment where women tell all the old stories
again and turn them inside-out and back-to-front – so the
characters you always thought were the goodies turn out to be the

147

baddies, and vice versa, and a whole lot of guilt is laid to rest: or that at least is the theory. I'm not sure myself that the guilt isn't just passed on to the next person, *in tacta*, so to speak. Certainly I want to carry and cope with my own guilt, because I want to carry and cope with my own virtue and I really don't see that you can have one without the other. Anyway, it would be hard to find a version of this story where I would come out a shiny new-style heroine: no true version, anyway. All I want to say is that it's more complicated, more complex, than it's told, and the reasons why it's told the way it is are complex too.

But I'm not willing to be a victim. I was not innocent, and I have grown out of innocence now and even out of wanting to be thought innocent. Living is a harsh business, as no one warned us when we were young and carefree under the apple bough, and I feel the weight of that ancient harshness and I want to embrace it, and not opt for some washed-out aseptic, hand-wringing, Disneyland garbage. (Though come to think of it he went none-too-easy on step-mothers, did he? Snow White's scared the socks off me the first time I saw the film – and partly of course because I recognised myself. But I digress.)

Look. It was like this. Or rather it was more like this, or parts of it were like this, or this is one part of it.

She was dead pretty in a Pears soap sort of way, and, honestly, terribly sweet and good. At first all I wanted her to do was concentrate. Concentration is the key to power. You have to concentrate on what is real. Concentration is not good or bad necessarily, but it is powerful. Enough power to change the world, that's all I wanted. (I was younger then, of course; but actually they're starving and killing whales and forests and each other out there; shutting your eyes and pretending they're not doesn't change anything. It does matter.) And what she was not was powerful. She wouldn't look out for herself. She was so sweet and so hopeful; so full of faith and forgiveness and love. You have to touch anger somewhere, rage even; you have to spit and roar and bite and scream and know it before you can be safe. And she never bloody would.

When I first married her father I thought she was so lovely, so

148

good and so sad. And so like her mother. I knew her mother very well, you see; we grew up together. I loved her mother. Really. With so much hope and fondness and awareness of her worth. But – and I don't know how to explain this without sounding like an embittered old bitch which I probably am – she was too good. Too giving. She gave herself away, indiscriminately. She didn't even give herself as a precious gift. She gave herself away as though she wasn't worth hanging on to. Generous to a fault, they said, when she was young, but no one acted as though it were a fault, so she never learned. 'Free with Kellogg's cornflakes' was her motto. She equated loving with suffering, I thought at one time, but that wasn't right, it was worse, she equated loving with being; as though she did not exist unless she was denying her existence. I mean, he was not a bad bloke, her husband, indeed I'm married to him myself, and I like him and we have good times together, but he wasn't worth it – no one is – not what she gave him, which was her whole self with no price tag on.

And it was just the same with that child. Yes, yes, one can understand: she had difficulty getting pregnant actually, she had difficulties carrying those babies to term too. Even I can guess how that might hurt. But her little girl was her great reward for suffering, and at the same time was also her handle on a whole new world of self-giving. And yes, of course she looked so lovely, who could have resisted her, propped up in her bed with that tiny lovely child sucking, sucking sucking? The mother who denied her little one nothing, the good mother, the one we all longed for, pouring herself out into the child. Well, I'll tell you, I've done it too, it is hell caring for a tiny daughter, I know. Everything, everything drags you into hell: the fact that you love and desire her, the fact that she's so needy and vulnerable, the fact that she never leaves you alone until your dreams are smashed in little piles and shabby with neglect, the fact that pleasure and guilt come so precisely together, as so seldom happens, working towards the same end and sucking your very selfhood out of you. It is a perilous time for a woman, that nursing of a daughter, and you can only survive it if you cling to yourself with a fierce and passionate love, *and* you back that up with a trained and militant lust for justice *and* you scream at the people around you to meet your needs and desires *and* you do not let them off, *and* when all is said and done you sit back and laugh at yourself with a well-timed and not unmalicious irony. Well, she could not, of course she could not, so she did not survive. She was never angry, she never asked, she took resignation – that tragic so-called virtue – as a ninth-rate alternative to reality and never even realised she had been short-changed.

So when I first married my husband I only meant to tease her a little, to rile her, to make her fight back. I couldn't bear it, that she was so like her mother and would go the same way. My girls were more like me, less agreeable to have about the house, but tough as old boots and capable of getting what they needed and not worrying too much about what they wanted or oughted, so to speak. I didn't have to worry about them. I just could not believe the sweetness of that little girl and her wide-eyed belief that I would be happy and love her if she would just deny herself and follow me. So of course I exploited her a bit, pushed and tested it, if you understand, because I couldn't believe it. Then I just wanted her to *see*, to see that life is not all sweetness and light, that people are not automatically to be trusted, that fairy godmothers are unreliable and damned thin on the ground, and that even the most silvery of princes soon goes out hunting and fighting and drinking and whoring, and doesn't give one tuppenny-ha'penny curse more for you than you give for yourself. Well, she could have looked at her father and known. He hardly proved himself to be the great romantic lover of all time, even at an age when that would have been appropriate, never mind later. He had after all replaced darling Mummy with me, and pretty damned quick too, and so long as he was getting his end off and his supper on the table he wasn't going to exert himself on her behalf, as I pointed out to her, by no means kindly.

(And, I should like to add, I still don't understand about that. I couldn't believe how little the bastard finally cared when it came to the point. Perhaps he was bored to tears by goodness, perhaps he was too lazy. He was a sentimental old fart about her, of course, his eyes could fill with nostalgic tears every time he looked at her and thought of her dead mother; but he never *did* anything; or even asked me to stop doing anything. She never asked, and he never had eyes to see, or energy or . . . God knows what went on in his head about her and as far as I'm concerned God's welcome. She loved him and trusted him and served him and he never even bloody noticed. Which sort of makes my point actually because he would never treat me like that, and yet he and I get on very well now; like each other and have good times in bed and out of it. Of course I'd never have let him tell me how to behave, but he might have tried, at least just once.)

Anyway, no, she would not see. She would not blame her father. She would not blame her mother, not even for dying, which is the ultimate outrage from someone you love. And she would not blame me. She just smiled and accepted, smiled and invented castles in the air to which someone, though never herself, would come and take her one day, smiled and loved me. No matter what I did to her, she just smiled.

So, yes, in the end I was cruel. I don't know how to explain it and I do not attempt to justify it. Her *wetness* infuriated me. I could not shake her good will, her hopefulness, her capacity to love and love and love such a pointless and even dangerous object. I could not make her hate me. Not even for a moment. I could not make her hate me. And I cannot explain what that frustration did to me. I hated her insane dog-like devotion where it was so undeserved. She treated me as her mother had treated him. I think I hated her stupidity most of all. I can hear myself almost blaming her for my belly-deep madness; I don't want to do that; I don't want to get into blaming the victim and she was my victim. I was older than her, and stronger than her, and had more power than her; and there was no excuse. No excuse, I thought the first time I ever hit her, but there was an excuse and it was my wild need, and it escalated.

So in the end – and yes I have examined all the motives and reasons why one woman should be cruel to another and I do not find them explanatory – so in the end I was cruel to her. I goaded and humiliated and pushed and bullied her. I used all my powers, my superior strength, my superior age, my superior intelligence, against her. I beat her, in the end, systematically and severely; but more than that I used her and worked her and

151

denied her pleasures and gave her pain. I violated her space, her dignity, her integrity, her privacy, even her humanity and perhaps her physical safety. There was an insane urge in me, not simply to hurt her, but to have her admit that I had hurt her. I would lie awake at night appalled, and scald myself with contempt, with anger and with self-disgust, but I had only to see her in the morning for my temper to rise and I would start again, start again at her with an unreasonable savagery that seemed to upset me more than it upset her. Picking, picking and pecking, endlessly. She tried my patience as no one else had ever done and finally I gave up the struggle and threw it away and entered into the horrible game with all my considerable capacity for concentration.

And nothing worked. I could not make her angry. I could not make her hate me. I could not stop her loving me with a depth and a generosity and a forgivingness that were the final blow. Nothing moved her to more than a simper. Nothing penetrated the fantasies and day dreams with which her head was stuffed so full I'm surprised she didn't slur her consonants. She was locked into perpetual passivity and gratitude and love. Even when she was beaten she covered her bruises to protect me; even when she was hungry she would not take food from my cupboards to feed herself; even when I mocked her she smiled at me tenderly.

All I wanted was for her to grow up, to grow up and realise that life was not a bed of roses and that she had to take some responsibility for her own life, to take some action on her own behalf, instead of waiting and waiting and waiting for something or someone to come shining out of the dark and force safety on her as I forced pain. What Someone? Another like her father who had done nothing, nothing whatever, to help her and never would? Another like him whom she could love generously and hopelessly and serve touchingly and givingly until weariness and pain killed her too. I couldn't understand it. Even when I beat her, even as I beat her, she loved me, she just loved and smiled and hoped and waited, day-dreamed and night-dreamed, and waited and waited and waited. She was untouchable and infantile. I couldn't save her and I couldn't damage her. God knows, I tried.

And now of course it's just an ancient habit. It has lost its sharp edges, lost the passion in both of us to see it out in conflict, between dream and reality, between hope and cynicism. There is a great weariness in me, and I cannot summon up the fire of conviction. I do not concentrate any more, I do not have enough concentration, enough energy, enough power. Perhaps she has won, because she drained that out of me years and years ago. Sometimes I despair, which wastes still more concentration. We plod on together, because we always have. Sweetly she keeps at it, smile, smile, dream, hope, wait, love, forgive, smile, smile, bloody smile. Tiredly, I keep at it too: 'Sweep that grate.' 'Tidy your room.' 'Do your homework.' 'What can you see in that nerd?' 'Take out those damn ear-phones and pay attention.' 'Life doesn't come free, you have to work on it.' 'Wake up, hurry up, stop day-dreaming, no you can't, yes you must, get a move on, don't be so stupid.' and 'You're not going to the ball, or party, or disco, or over your Nan's, dressed like *that*.'

She calls it nagging.

She calls me Mummy.

'LET US NOW PRAISE UNKNOWN WOMEN AND OUR MOTHERS WHO BEGAT US'

— ⚮ —

It was the apples that did it.

The smell of warm apples, because in the weary muddle of the evening before she had left the bag of apples too near the radiator; and the memories, released, surged into the dark room and wrapped her as tenderly in their arms as she wrapped her baby.

No one had warned her, or rather, yes they had but she had not been able to hear any warnings. The utter exhaustion, the disorienting lack of sleep, the constancy of demand, those things she had more or less anticipated. But the debilitating draining passion of love she had not been prepared for; nor the sense of being laid too wide open, spread out too thin, her sense of personal boundaries destroyed, the confusion of self and other, the exposure of body and thought both to the use of another and not even knowing when it had become another not a part of herself. Worse, worse even than being-in-love, an experience she had always found uncomfortable and self-annihilating because the object and the source of the passion, the self-destruction and the confusion, was both utterly vulnerable to her and utterly ungiving. She had woken and slept and listened and organised and suffered physically and slaved and poured out the resources of her own body, blood and milk and time and energy, for six unrelenting weeks of service to someone who gave nothing in return, nothing at all except the physical fact of its existence. The baby took, and took and took and took, long after she had nothing left to give and still she does not hate but loves the baby, passionately, tear-jerkingly and finally, wearily, bitterly, defeatedly, and this was the third time in five hours that she had been dragging awake, her dreams smashed, fragmented, stolen, sucked down with the milk into the maw of that all-consuming, tyrannical, tiny, powerful, beautiful body.

And then she catches the smell of apples, and sitting on the dark sofa with her daughter sucking, sucking, sucking, she spins away out across the galaxies of time and memory and smells afresh apples in a warm cupboard, tastes the strange cleanness of elderflower tea, touches the soft roughness of old linen curtains, hears the clear note of a flute playing in a next-door room, sees beautiful orange dragons on delicate china cups and knows herself, long legs in shorts, bony, awkward, lost, waylaid temporarily on her certain journey through childhood. Ten or eleven years young; unkempt, not physically but emotionally, lonely, fierce, on holiday with her mother and her mother's new lover; husband and child replaced. Husband rightly, the daughter knew, but herself *wrongly*, and dangerously and what certainty can there ever be again and a great passion of anger and injustice and trying-to-be-good and sulking instead. And too much, 'Why don't you go out and play darling,' and, 'Go on, darling, don't mope around so, the fresh air is good for you,' and, 'Do go out and enjoy yourself, darling, you don't need to wait for us, we don't mind.'

So she had moped around through the first half of a hot and lovely country August. To amuse herself she took to spying on other people, listening to the chatter at the counter of the village shop, lurking behind the bus stop and peering in through windows. She bought herself a notebook and filled it with mean sketches and vicious reports on all the people; and nobody liked her very much and none of the other children wanted to play with her because she was not very nice at all. She speculated for her victims' lives of dreariness and small-mindedness and believed in the objectivity of her own observations so she did not even want them to like her, because they were not very nice people anyway.

She extended her researches to the edge of the village. Up a small track there was a cottage with a lovely garden and behind

the garden a wooded slope with undergrowth and one morning
she decided to hide up there and see what she could see. A hot
sunny morning, and the garden with rough grass, not a lawn,
which ran under fruit trees and around casual flower beds down
to the green back door. And after a little while a big, fat, old
woman came out of the door and started weeding in the garden.
She turned her back on the slope and leaned down to pull weeds,
leaning from the waist with her legs apart, barely thirty feet away.
And the enormousness of her bottom sticking up, the rest of her
trunk and head invisible, huge and fat and disgusting, her floppy
tweed skirt stretched wide and held by the huge knees, ungainly,
ugly and, from the vantage point in the undergrowth, splendidly
ludicrous. So she whipped out her notebook and was about to
sketch that enormous bottom and write some telling comments
on it and its owner when, without looking up and without
turning round, the gardening woman said, very loudly, 'Don't
you dare.' And without thinking she had shoved away the
notebook and said, 'What?' 'Don't you dare write any comments
on how hideous and silly I look here.' And the woman straightened up but still did not turn round, her hair was escaping wispily
from its bun, and she still looked silly and ugly, her cardigan was
baggy too. 'Come down here.'

She had been frightened then, embarrassed and scared,
convinced that the woman would demand to see the notebook;
but she tried not to let it show, hopped over the garden fence
jauntily, and with a moderately successful assumption of effront-
ery strolled down the garden. But the woman did not demand or
ask anything, she just smiled and said, 'My name's Elaine, what's
yours?' The smile undid her jauntiness. 'Clare,' she muttered,
shifting from leg to leg. Elaine said, 'Well, if my legs are too fat,
yours are too thin. Do you like our garden?' And without
touching her she showed Clare round the garden telling her the
names of the flowers and pointing out interesting things that were
happening – rose suckers and old nests and ripening fruit. She
never mentioned the notebook. Emboldened, Clare finally
asked, 'How did you know? I mean, that I was there, and about
the notebook?' 'O, I'm a witch,' said Elaine calmly. 'My friend is
too; and we have a cat as our familiar, which everyone thinks is

called Smudge, but whose real name is Thunder-flower.' She
was not laughing at Clare and Clare knew it. Elaine said, 'Why
don't you come in and meet the others?' And they had gone quite
comfortably through the green door and into the kitchen. From
the front of the house she could hear a flute playing, and Elaine
said, 'That's Isobel but she'll finish practising in a minute; in the
meantime if you look in that cupboard you'll find three blue
mugs. Could you get them out while I boil the kettle?' And while
Clare was looking in the cupboard which was full of different-
coloured mugs and plates, not proper sets like her mother had but
different colours and sizes, some of them old and fine and some
of them modern pottery and some just plastic, and getting out the
three blue ones, the flute-playing stopped and Elaine put her
head out of the kitchen and called, 'Isobel, we've got a visitor.'
Isobel, who was very tall and not much older than Clare's
mother, but much messier and wearing the sort of crimplene
slacks that her mother would not have been seen dead in, came
into the kitchen and looked at her and said, 'How do you do?'
Not kindly to a child, but properly. She didn't seem to be at all
surprised to see a strange child in her kitchen, but smiled and said
to Elaine, 'I have had such a lovely practice, it was really sweet of
you to go outside while I tried the frilly bits.' Then she reached
down a tin from a high shelf and opened it and put it, half-full of
biscuits, on the kitchen table. The kettle boiled and Elaine made
the tea and she had sat with them at the wobbly table and they
had chatted. And the women had asked no finding-out questions,
they had just let her be and join in or not as she wanted. And
when she realised that it was nearly lunchtime she said that she
ought to go and they took her through to the front of the house
and let her out of the front door very politely. When she was
halfway down the path Isobel called out, 'We hope you'll be able
to come again. Any time you want to, drop in. You haven't met
Thunder-flower yet.' And Elaine added, 'We need an apprentice
anyway.' And when she got back to the cottage they were staying
in she was not in a sulk any more, but she did not tell her mother
where she had been all morning because she wanted to keep it as
her own secret. She did not want her mother going and getting
friendly with them.

And for the last two weeks of her holiday she went there nearly every day. They didn't do anything very exciting; they taught her how to make jam, how to care for the garden, how to store apples, each one having its own space and not having to touch the others. They gave her homemade elderflower tea to drink, a cool taste with a sharp touch somewhere, not like anything else she'd ever tasted. Isobel played on the flute and Elaine accompanied her on the piano and taught Clare how to turn the pages. Sometimes Elaine read stories to her and Thunder-flower coiled around her shoulders when she sat in the big armchair; and what they had done, though she did not know it then, was pay exquisite attention to her in the simple assumption that she was worthy of attention, that she was a nice and clever person, not a small and ferocious animal. So she told them lots of things that she had never told anyone else, and they listened and discussed them and were interested, but not pushy. She told them about school, and her friends at home and how she did not want to go and live in a new poky flat instead of her old home; she told them about the divorce, and how her father did not talk to people and was sad and grouchy, and about Ben who was nicer than that and how that made her feel bad, and about how angry she was with her mother and how she hated her and loved her and how it all hurt so much. And telling it aloud didn't make it feel better exactly but it did help it to make sense. They listened and respected her and liked her. She was too young even to wonder why; she was just happy and useful there, with them and they were happy and useful with each other, and she could see that. It was true that they were witches and she knew it, although Isobel pretended to be a school teacher and Elaine pretended to be a retired school teacher, and Thunder-flower pretended to be a sweet little pussycat called Smudge; and if she had not known she would never have guessed that she came in from nightprowling with blood on her paws and wild green eyes. The flowers grew in their garden, the copper shone in their fireplace, the irregular weave of their curtains changed colour from minute to minute and the smell of apples pervaded the whole cottage. And one day when they had all been chopping up logs in the garden and Clare had helped carry them down to the wood shed she saw their two

broom sticks leaning against the shed wall and had felt a shiver of
excitement. Two well-made besom brooms, one slightly thicker
in the handle than the other, and their delicate fingery twigs
spreading out and casting tangly clear shadows from the afternoon sun on to the dusty walls of the wood shed.

Her mother and Ben had been only too glad to have her
happier and calmer and busier, so they did not ask too many
questions. The weight was removed and she flourished in the
freer air. Once, when her mother had planned a well-intentioned
and guilt-absolving picnic on the beach and Clare had casually
rejected it in favour of one more day with Elaine and Isobel, her
mother exclaimed in exasperation, 'Whatever do you do there all
day? What's so special about two old ladies and a cat?' But Clare
did not answer because she did not know. She was careful
though, careful not to tell her mother they were witches, because
a witches' apprentice never gives her teachers away. Sometimes
they burned witches on bonfires, so she knew she had to be
careful.

The holiday came to an end. She went the last day, sadly, to
say goodbye to them, to try and say thank you for a gift she knew
even then she had been given without knowing what it was. They
had tea together, not in the blue mugs but in some beautiful
delicate china cups with orange dragons on them; not at the
kitchen table but in the sitting-room, and although it was not
cold they had lit the fire for her. There was cinnamon toast and
fat fruit cake with nuts in. Isobel poured slowly, carefully, from a
silver teapot. They had made tea special for her, ritualised,
timeless, because she was their friend. When it was nearly time
to go, Elaine had looked her straight in the eye and said, 'You
know, I think you should leave that notebook with us. You know
we will never never read it, but we would keep it safe; furious,
mean thoughts need to be kept safe. We will put a very firm,
strong, good spell on it.' And she had taken it out of her pocket
and given it to them without a qualm. Isobel said, 'Of course, we
will replace it for you.' They gave her another notebook, small
and covered in bottle-green watered silk, and the pages were old
and creamy, heavy, soft, and they had no lines, just blank so she
could write and draw whatever she chose. It was ancient and

beautiful. 'It's a spell book,' said Elaine. 'You can of course put
in anything you want, but try only to make strong, hopeful spells
if you can. It is all right to do angry spells, but not mean ones or
despairing ones. Remember – "Hope has two lovely daughters –
anger and courage". Witches always take responsibility for what
they do. They are loyal and loving and hopeful.'

'Have you made me a witch now?' she asked.

'No,' said Elaine, 'nobody can ever make anyone a witch, but
you can be one any time you want to. You just have to believe it,
that's all. You just say, "I am a witch," and you will be. You can
even fly if you want to, but you have to believe in your own
power. You see, it's very easy.' She smiled and Clare smiled
back. 'Oh, and by the way, you don't need to have a broomstick,
that's completely optional. All you need is to remember that you
are a witch woman, full of power and strength, and then you can
do anything you want. You can make things and break things and
call storms and grow plants and heal people and hurt people. It's
up to you.'

And a little later she had gone down the path in the long light
of the afternoon, leaving them standing arm in arm in their
cottage doorway. She had been completely and perfectly happy,
warm tea and toast in her tummy, warm love and power in her
stomach. The next day she and her mother and Ben had driven
away and she had gone back to school and forgotten. She had
forgotten. But now, feeding her new daughter in the depths of the
night, she remembered. She remembered not just the happen-
ings of that summer, but absolutely the taste and touch and sight
and smell and sound of them. She remembered her own nervous
embarrassment when Elaine had called her from the garden; and
how comfortable it had been with the two of them. She felt again
how it was to be a perfectly and absolutely happy child, and knew
again the power and goodness of being a strong woman.

So, now, she laid the sleeping baby on the sofa beside her, and
wedged her in with a handy cushion, because a witch always
takes responsibility for what she does, and she walked over to the
window and opened it. The moon, on its wane, rode the
shoulder of a cloud and illuminated its frilled edges; the air was
cool and milky. She said, 'I am a witch. I can make things and

161

break things, and call storms and grow plants and babies and heal
people and hurt people. I believe in my power. I can fly.' In her
cotton nightdress she clambered on to the window sill and leapt
out into the waiting air. After the first delighted surprise at
finding that it really worked, she soared upwards, dancing upon
the darkness, and testing her twists and turns. Steering was more
problematic than she had imagined, but by no means impossible.
She alighted briefly in the tree opposite her window to thank it for
its beauty and generosity which she did not always remember to
notice, then she flew back to the window to check on the baby.
She was sleeping sweetly, the fluff on her head poking upwards
and her long lashes folded downwards on her cheek. So Clare
turned and left her and flew over London; a strange new and
magical city seen from the air – Primrose Hill a tiny paradise with
little lampstands and the playground sheltering under the huge
spider's web of the Bird House in Regent's Park. St Pancras
Station was a fairy-tale castle, turreting and cavorting outrage-
ously in the moonlight, and the great dome of St Paul's a loving
and protective breast. She swooped now, moving with certainty
in her new element, and rose to greet the stars, and swung low
over the streets of the City, deserted and ancient and longing for
her visitation. She shot out over the river and flew upwards to
watch it snake its glittery way across the town. She darted from
side to side, delighting; the bridges were garlands, garlands of fire,
linking the two heavier masses of earth across the deep of water;
and the air embraced them all. She was perfectly and absolutely
happy, and knew the power and the goodness of being a strong
woman.

And as she flew downstream towards the docks and Greenwich
she began to sing a deep new song, and she called on all other
witches everywhere to come and sing it with her, and they came.
Elaine and Isobel, still smiling, and a woman who lived four
doors down from her at home and whose fierce purposeful
striding had always filled Clare with fear; and the middle-aged
woman who guarded the changing rooms at her local swimming
pool and whose shiny black skin rippled gloriously in the
moonlight; and the midwife who had delivered her daughter and
hauled her through the confusion of pain and emotion. And

more and more women, thrusting beautiful, confident bodies
through the new air and singing, singing, singing her song with
her. And flying over the river more fun than she could have
dreamed: Formation Flying, as funny and silly and skilful as the
women on *Come Dancing*; and Free Fall, where there is no
gravity but only perfect dignity; and Pairs, more sensuous and
tender than terrestrial dancing can ever approach; and Exhibi-
tionism, solo flights and stunts of daring and careening wildness
and mutual admiration; and just being there, flying, dancing
with crazy, immodest, hysterical, free laughter and song. 'Welcome to the Coven,' laughed a woman just below her and she
looked down and it was her science mistress from school, who
grinned and adjusted her white overall and not for the sake of
decency. There were women she recognised from history books
and portrait galleries and women she had never seen before, and
young and old and in-between and witches' dancing-skins come
in more colours than the rainbow. And the trying soreness that
still irritated her vagina from where she had been stitched after
the birth was soothed and healed by the soft air, so she tugged off
her nightie and laughed as it floated like a tiny pale cloud down
into the river beneath. Turning deftly in the air she saw her
stretch marks as silvery-purple bands of strength which glowed
pearly in the moonlight. And she was full of joy.

And later she flew quietly home, leaving the radiant dancers,
fliers, singers; because after childbirth a witch knows she needs a
certain amount of quiet and solitude so that she can learn again
what are her boundaries, and a certain amount of rest because
caring for a small baby is very demanding; and witches always
take responsibility for what they do. She rested after her pleasing
exertions in the green tree outside her home and when she felt
perfectly comfortable she flew back in through the window and
alighted. Her daughter was still asleep, tidily on her tummy on
the sofa, and the delicate hair which fringed the rims of her ears
seemed to glow in the moonlight. Clare picked her up carefully
and was about to carry her safely back to her basket in the
bedroom when the baby opened her eyes, awakened but not
frightened by the cool softness of Clare's naked·body. Four eyes
very close to one another and glowing in the dark like cats'. And

the baby was so quiet, so present, so softly smelling of warm milk,
so beautiful, so perfect, so courageous and bold a decision against
such impossibly long odds, so little and funny, that Clare could
not help but smile. She murmured, 'You little witch, daughter of
a witch, you can be a witch too if you want to. Remember that.'
And in the quiet of the ending of the night, the daughter, for the
very first time, smiled back.

PARTICLES OF A WAVE.
AN AFTERWORD

%

So I rang the commissioning editor to discuss this essay, and how it could best explain everything: me, life, what I write, and the world in general. She wanted me to say something about Faith (on being a Christian and why God is important to me) in – I quote – 'some innovative form'. I wanted to do something on why children are such a crucial positive asset to me as a woman writer. I argued forcibly that this has a lot to do with Faith (Does it? I wondered, panicked). We seemed to be approaching possible agreement. Then she said, 'You will put in something about being a vicar's wife, won't you? After all, that is what most people find interesting about you.'

Appalled, writhing, I terminated the conversation cravenly. Then I felt depressed.

Why? I mean, why so depressed? I am after all married to a vicar and people do find this interesting. Well, partly of course because it is not a nice feeling to be defined by your spouse's job. (Spouse is bloody cheating, actually; men are very seldom defined by their wife's job; this is an issue of sexism.) But . . . but also . . . I really do not like the image of the 'charming and eccentric artist', however presented. It is a dangerous trap for both the artist and the consumer. I cannot help feeling that it is perceived as suitably batty that I should be a Christian at all, for a feminist writer to be a vicar's wife is splendidly part of that way of perceiving writers (it is also, in fairness, splendidly part of that way of perceiving vicars, but that has to be his problem). I know all about it because I do it myself; I play up to the complexities of my own life; I feed on the tremor of curiosity I can generate just by giving my address. But that does not mean I like it. I don't. I don't say 'artist' any more; I don't even say 'writer' often – though putting it on my passport after years of 'researcher' was a great liberation for me. I try to say 'worker in cultural production', although it sticks like heavy toffee on my tongue. I don't believe in the contemporary stereotypes of the artist, and I don't think they are useful. Incidentally, I am a vicar's wife.

A quote from Borges.

Thinking, analysing, inventing are not anomalous acts; they are the normal respiration of the intelligence. To glorify the occasional performance of that function, to hoard ancient and alien thoughts, to recall with incredulous stupor what the doctor universalis *thought, is to confess to our laziness or our barbarity. Every man should be capable of all ideas and I understand that in the future this will be the case.*

(Should I cheat here and re-translate 'man' as 'person'? I don't read Spanish, so I don't know. It does matter.)

Life it seems to me is a pretty messy business. Within an untimable matter of minutes, later the same evening, I decide:

i) that I can't won't write such an essay at all;

ii) that we will have spaghetti for supper (again);

iii) that it will *probably* be safe for my son to play with the liquidiser;

iv) that as there are 10,789 Anglican priests in the Church's full-time employment, there must be about 7,250 wives (the Church Information Office to their credit could not be more precise): I am neither representative nor atypical of them;

v) that I would like to write a story about Judith and Holofernes – chopping off heads seems to meet my own mood just now;

vi) that as there are no tinned tomatoes we will have fish fingers for supper instead (again);

vii) a) that my son is so beautiful it would be a pity if he mangled his fingers; I will dedicate my next volume of short stories to him instead (cf. acknowledgements); and consequent on his response to this loving decision;

b) child murder is an entirely justified social good which should be funded by the State. I will write a story with Herod as the hero;

viii) I will write the essay after all.

I also, while clearing up the puppy's soggy paper, read an old article that says that women can't be great chess players because they have too many 'interrupt factors' – i.e. they can't concentrate. This may of course be true (although the author did not ask why and did not point out that there are very few men great chess players either) but I don't want to be a great chess player so it hardly matters.

Just after York Minster was struck by lightning I was on my way to the post office when I met an elderly woman. She was distressed by this bolt from the heavens, this 'act of God', as the insurance people call it. Did I think, she asked, that God had done it on purpose, as some of the newspapers were speculating? The post was about to leave, and I was in a hurry, but how can anyone resist such a question? No, I said, I didn't think so, did she? No, she said, she didn't think God was like that. There was a pause, and I was poised to escape. Then she added with a tone of affectionate criticism, 'But he should have been more careful, he should have *known* there'd be talk.'

And the whole day flashed with glory. That is my theology exactly (well, almost exactly because as a good feminist I don't think of God as 'he'). God is not malicious, but careless, random, extravagant, indiscriminate. I don't base what Faith I have on the feeling of 'what a friend I have in Jesus', but on that continual, inescapable sense of the power and the mystery and the danger and the profligacy of it all. I mean *all*, from the bizarre goings-on inside each atom – wave function and proton exchange and reverse time – right through to the social complexity of history and class and gender and race and individual experience.

The Church and the Great Novel both try to structure that intellectually and emotionally, both to contain and to reveal it.

Form, it is called, form and structure and genre. I cling to orthodoxy in theology and to form in cultural production. The challenge is to go as near to the edge, as near to the power and the mystery and the danger, without collapsing into chaos. We need as many counterweights, as many interrupt factors as we can lay our hands on. Neither the Great Novel nor the Church seem to be working too well at the moment. We just catch the fragments as best we can – but it is all one chaos, I think, though differently delineated, represented.

This morning I took the post out into our lovely garden. (Look, I live in the most delightful seventeen-roomed Victorian Gothic fantasy, with a curved and secret garden and enough space for all of us not to hear each other crying at night unless we want to. I love it. I live in it solely and only because I am a vicar's wife. It is not irrelevant.) Both the children are playing under the lawn sprinkler in the bright sunshine. Mildred has reached a new place of self-consciousness and does not play naked. Adam, like his namesake, is unashamed. They are pure energy, extremely demanding, and this morning at least completely physically delightful. They dance in the water and I am enchanted, seduced. This morning I was meant to be upstairs, drafting a short story. It is not their demandingness that keeps me from this sterner pleasure, but their loveliness. I have written before about how their dailiness and iron will for my attention balance and protect me against the dangerous voyages of the imagination – they ballast me safely with normality and connectedness, and ensure my return to sanity and to home. I have not written about the reverse: how the rigour and excitement and challenge of writing fiction weights me against their enchantment, against maternal romanticism and the isolated womb life in the garden.

I examined my post, a little dreamily: two bills, a set of minutes from a meeting, a circular and a long letter from my agent, immensely supportive and helpful, but wondering if I wouldn't like to write another 'proper' novel soon and if I could consider slipping in a few 'ordinary' people (I have a nasty feeling that this means no God and no lesbian nuns and a few more men) and a touch more social realism – class and things like that. And she says, 'Living in your vicarage, you know this enormous range of people.' Which is true, I suppose. I look at the children who are perfectly ordinary, as well as beautiful, and one of whom is, in the meaning of the word, a man. And I look at the ordinary roses blooming (and cannot help noting to myself that I must ring Joyce – a very ordinary friend of mine – and tell her she can come and cut some for the church on Sunday/); and at the ordinary minutes from my meeting on Values in British Society chaired by the Archbishop of York; and at the dead ordinary bills – gas and car insurance, as it happens; and I don't want to write about any of these things. Or rather I think I do write about them all the time. They are both protection and the way in. It is because of them, and the bittiness of everything – and I mustn't forget to take the parish minibus to be serviced this week – that I can write stories about magic and find beauty in all the truly dreadful things that do happen.

Over 10 per cent of all known life forms are directly parasitic; mothers cut up their daughters' genitalia with broken bottles; ordinary 'sane' men beat their wives to a pulp and cannot understand that there is anything wrong with this; witches burn; the Government wants to cut the ILEA budget while over 29 per cent of the children in our local primary school have learning or behavioural difficulties. Never mind about bombs and famines and imperialism (though I do mind).

I don't see how I could write Social Realism, about ordinary people, without going insane.

A quote from Annie Dillard.

I have never understood why so many mystics of all creeds experience the presence of God on mountain tops. Aren't they afraid of being blown away? God said to Moses on Sinai that even the priests who have access to the Lord must hallow themselves for fear that the Lord will break out against them. This is the fear. It often feels best to lie low, inconspicuous, instead of waving your spirit around from high places like a lightning rod. For if God is in one sense the igniter, a fireball that spins over the ground of continents, God is also the destroyer, lightning, blind power, impartial as the atmosphere . . . You get a comforting sense in a curved hollow place of being vulnerable to only a narrow column of God as air.

The washing machine broke down yesterday, and the man (*sic*) can't come and fix it till next week. I am trying to learn to remember my dreams, and when I woke up yesterday morning I thought I was getting somewhere, but somehow Adam managed to shut himself in his bedroom and started screaming, not in fear which one might have comforted, but in pure bloody bad temper; and this failed to wake the Vicar who slept on sweetly. Also, one of the kids from the parish stole some cash from the kitchen, and I wish I didn't know which one it was. And my mother rang up worrying about the children's education which she seriously doubts can happen within the state system. And someone wondered whether I could please possibly take their TV to the menders (she's old, she's housebound, she needs the TV and I am privileged to have the only car in the parish family). And this collection of short stories is nearly due and is not finished and I desire it to be good. And I wanted so much to see a dear friend of mine who's leaving – lucky woman – for six weeks in the USA. And someone who is on a committee I'm on rang up wanting me to bully the chairman (*sic*), quite rightly as it happens, but she said, 'But, Sara, you're so good at being rude to people.' And . . . and . . . and it is out of all this that the stories come and do not some without, but at the same time it is impossibly hard to accept that these are useful incursions into my time/space. If it is mine.

The poet Helen Sands told me once that giving birth was, for her, like being God. Being me, I thought she meant the power and the creativity, but she said, 'No, no. I mean it is just being *now*. You're just doing totally what you're doing. I think that must be it – the totalness of it. Being the centre of the world, and that is how we could be all the time presumably but we're not; this thing of just not being distracted anywhere, totally in yourself, totally present to what is happening. And it is mysterious. This mysterious life you are going to meet, that is going to come out of you. It's a great work that has to be done, I mean it isn't on a plate this great work that has to be done to give birth,

170

this "groaning and travail". But it's funny because it is so ordinary too . . . it was just ordinary, we were just doing a job – and that in itself was whatever was needed.'

One of the novices in our local convent took her Life Vows last month. (An Art Form if ever there was one in the 1980s.) The Vicar and I spend the evening before creating a nun's habit out of bits of felt and cord and fitting it to a gin bottle as a present for her (a very creative, artistic act: the form imposed by historical tradition within rigorous boundaries, only the interpretation of the material to be discovered). We were tickled by the result, and pleased with ourselves and her. Professions – the formal taking of vows – are not that common these days, far less common than being a vicar's wife or writing a novel. It was a lovely ceremony. I really wanted to ask her if she embraced the structures of the religious life as a way to limit the amount of God crashing in on her, or if the formal requirements were a way to find space to reveal her own truth. I also wanted to ask her how far I was allowed to use her experience, or my experience of her experience? What are the boundaries of ownership? What are the stuffs of fiction? Perhaps I will ask her one sometime. Later the same day I went out to have a drink with a friend. How, I asked her, does she choose the structures of her life? What creates the boundaries? What keeps her power and her energy channelled, grounded? At first she was baffled by the questions, then she said, 'Sex.' We grinned. But that was real too, a real part of it all. Before I had the children and started writing for a living I used to sew a lot – tiny, detailed petit-point. In her book *On Gender and Writing*, Michelene Wandor notes the same thing: when she went back to college and temporarily stopped imaginative production she took up embroidery. Once Mildred was born, once Michelene finished her degree, we both stopped. The desire evaporated. People jog, play musical instruments, cook meals, work in their gardens, make love, dye their hair, get up in the mornings. These things are usually called by that faintly derogatory term – Hobbies: only if they conform to certain structures, certain mythologies, are they called Art and the 'artists' are glorified, iconised; also cut off, isolated. Of course I know

171

ordinary people, everyone knows ordinary people. We are all ordinary people. At the imaginative level the artists aren't allowed to be ordinary people, and not knowing the dailiness, the ordinariness of creative activity they have to put it all into their work and you get trite mysticism or dreary old social realism again. The same things happen to too many mothers as a matter of fact: iconised and isolated – and you get trite earth-goddess or dreary exhaustion. Alcohol/Valium; eccentricity/depression; recluse/bad-tempered nag – they look suspiciously alike. These things have to belong to more people, and individuals have to have access to more of them.

So my friend and I got drunk and then I went home to bed.

I have been reading or trying to read about the new physics recently. I thought there was something there, something that might help unite fiction and non-fiction, imagination and matter. I still think there is. But I also thought it might discipline my fragmented mind. Instead it has boggled it. Everything seems woolly, imprecise. And I have scared myself. A student once complained to his eminent professor that he did not understand something in theory and was told, 'Young man, in mathematics you do not understand things, you just get used to them.' This does not immediately strike one as a very clarifying, radical or transformatory notion. What if it is true? I do not like the idea. I do not like the idea of Heisenberg's Uncertainty Principle either, which says that you cannot simultaneously know where something is *and* how fast it is going somewhere else. One or the other with precision, but not both.

Do I want to make it all too simple? Trying to argue that all the whirling particles are united, do belong to and nourish each other, but that at the same time we cannot locate them all at once, and determine how soon they will be somewhere different. That it is only in the split second of collision that the sparks fly wildly and make enough light to see. The centre holds, but does not hold still long enough to be certain. One has to take the magical moment of improbability and argue probability from it. Focusing on one 'observable' tends to blur the others: individual freedoms clang resoundingly into social justices. Emphasising psychological factors seems to paralyse political analysis. Belief in God reduces social responsibility. Yes, there is something holy and magical about writing books and having babies and sex and religious vows and the social complexity of the tower block and playing in the garden. And no, there is nothing magical about any of them, they are ordinary historical events, culturally determined: production, reproduction and life styles. 'You have to separate in order to unite,' the novelist Michele Roberts once argued with me. But how do you know you can ever unite it all at all, I want to ask, when it all moves so fast, and the sum of the parts adds up to something quite different from the whole?

Once I had some women friends round for supper and we were all bitching about life and meaning and other such high-minded things and how we really deserved better from the universe than we seemed to be getting. Afterwards my daughter said to me, 'I'm not going to be like you lot when I grow up.' I was afraid we might have depressed her. 'Why not?' I asked. 'Because you don't know how to make choices.'

I do know that my life is fragmented. I do lots of things, I do them and so in some ways I am them: mothering, theology, friendship, writing, studying, gossiping, washing up, driving the parish minibus, vicar's wifing, cooking, worrying, dreaming and politicking. (Nor should you overlook both the deliberately and the accidentally omitted fragments, incidentally.) And I live in a fragmented universe too. But I do not want to be a great chess player – they all seem totally deranged.

Now:
    Are these fragments the splinters of glass in a kaleidoscope which form and reform and make patterns, which although constantly changing are none the less organised and pleasing? If so, the more fragments the greater the possibility of complexity and beauty – the more the merrier.
    Or: do women's lives obey the rule of wave/particle duality. 'The language of quantum theory is precise but tricky. Quantum

theory does not state that something – like light, for example – can be wave-like and particle-like *at the same time*. According to Bohr's complementarity, light reveals either a particle-like aspect or a wave-like aspect depending on the context (i.e. the experiment). It is not possible to observe both the wave-like aspect and the particle-like aspect in the same situation. *However, both these mutually exclusive aspects are needed to understand 'light'.* In this sense light is both particle-like and wave-like.' (Gary Zukav.)

Or: Is the whole thing just fragmented chaos? Does the Old Man throw dice?

Look, all these suggestions are only images anyway. I just wanted to explain why I have spent the last year writing short stories about magic and congruence and things.

SARA MAITLAND AND
MICHELENE WANDOR

ARKY TYPES

Dear Reader,

The writing of novels in letter form has a long and
honourable literary pedigree.

Now ARKY TYPES ventures where no epistolary novel
has gone before, by introducing the letters of two popular
contemporary writers – Sara Maitland and Michelene
Wandor – alongside those of nuns, dancers, camel-tamers,
publishers, vicars' wives and Jewish mothers, unicorns,
policewomen, literary agents and worms.

Here you will find flamboyant feminism, wild wit,
stirring stories and an inventive and extraordinary
examination of the process of writing fiction.

Who wrote which letters? Is it fact or is it fiction? Explore
the intriguing correspondence of ARKY TYPES and jump
to your own conclusions.

Happy reading.
Yours,
The Fiction Editor, Methuen.

VIVIAN GLOVER

THE FIRST FIG TREE

At the back of a house in one of the Southern States of
America, a great-grandmother passes the time in her
rocking chair under the shade of a large pecan tree. But her
tranquillity is broken when she admits into her company
her great-granddaughter, left behind while her parents
pursue the war effort. Both refusing to admit to loneliness,
they are nevertheless drawn together by stories about the
great-grandmother's past which began in slavery; and
together – against the entrenched harshness of the
segregationist South – they try to understand the events
around them, affecting people they know and, eventually,
themselves.

'A compassionate and perceptive debut novel told by a
refreshing new voice'
Time Out

'Very moving indeed'
New Statesman

'Deserves a wide readership'
Mail on Sunday

'A touching novel in which black women achieve an
autonomy denied to whites and men in general'
City Limits

NAWAL EL SAADAWI

SHE HAS NO PLACE IN PARADISE

A groom is filled with dread at his approaching wedding ceremony in which his manhood will be tested; his fear of his mother turns to fear and hatred for the young unknown bride he is obliged to marry. This story of power and impotence is the first in a new collection which brilliantly exposes the relationships between individuals in today's society. A man is terrified to speak the truth to men more powerfully placed than he; a woman knows nothing of the feelings her well-bred husband's friend has for her; discovering her emerging sexuality a teenager battles with her adoration and fear of her father; a worker, when tortured for information, triumphantly discovers that the essential core of himself can withdraw and survive . . .

Written by one of Egypt's leading writers, this latest volume of subtle, sharp stories on sexual politics follows Nawal El Saadawi's excellent earlier volume, *Death of an Ex-Minister*, about which reviewers commented:

'Nicely judged and chilling in their matter-of-factness'
City Limits

'Highly tuned political instincts . . . fascinating characters'
Guardian

'Powerful stories that are written simply and directly, making them all the more poignant and startling'
Women's Review

'They're brilliant . . . The writing is subtle and sensitive and the translation is excellent.'
Publishing News

'A collection of remarkably controlled, provocative and well-written stories'
Venue

JULIA VOZNESENSKAYA

THE STAR CHERNOBYL

The Star Chernobyl is a powerful and timely novel about one of the world's worst disasters, as seen through the eyes of three Russian sisters.

Anna is in Sweden when the disaster occurs. Increasingly anxious to understand the truth in the face of conflicting media reports, she tries to contact her sister Anastasia to learn the true nature of events. The third sister, Alenka, is working in Chernobyl; and it is intense concern for her well-being which provokes Anastasia's determination to find her. As she enters the 'Dead Zone' of Chernobyl, events and characters become more desperate and bizarre, while Anastasia's mission assumes tragic proportions.

The Star Chernobyl is a devastating critique of government-controlled media, as well as a sympathetic portrayal of how the human spirit tries to triumph over cataclysmic events, even when struggling against the denial of basic freedoms. Following her success with *The Women's Decameron*, Julia Voznesenskaya has written an astonishing novel whose subject cannot fail both to move and disturb.

'*The Star Chernobyl* is intense and memorable – not Tolstoy but eminently worthy of its terrible topic'
London Review of Books

MICHELE ROBERTS

THE BOOK OF MRS NOAH

'A woman visiting Venice with her pre-occupied husband
fantasizes that she is Mrs Noah. The Ark is a vast library, a
repository not only of creatures but of the entire knowledge
and experience of the human race. She is its curator (or
'Arkivist'), and her fellow voyagers are a group of five Sibyls
and a single man, the Gaffer, a bearded old party who once
wrote a best-selling book and has now retired to a tax heaven
in the sky. Each Sibyl tells a story and each story is about
the way men have oppressed women down the centuries.

'I have not felt so uneasy and so guilty about my gender
since I read Margaret Atwood's *The Handmaid's Tale*. To
say that *The Book of Mrs Noah* is a superb novel sounds
impertinent or patronizing. But it remains the case'
Kenneth McLeish, *Daily Telegraph*

'Sharply but sympathetically observed . . . both down to
earth and visionary. Roberts' writing is rich, troubling and
audacious . . . the female imagination at its best'
City Life

'A feast of inventive imagery . . . it's not unusual for a
woman writer to pitch for brave humour, but to strike the
note as truly as Roberts does is a marvel'
Company

'A strange and interesting book, pouring the subject matter
of Virginia Woolf into a form designed by Boccaccio'
Independent

'Like the best of new women's writing, takes a generous
view of the widely different ways in which women find their
salvation, and avoids feminist clichés . . . a poetic,
visionary book, and humorous as well'
Cosmopolitan

'A slow, rich read of pleasurable complexity'
Guardian

BARBARA COMYNS

MR FOX

Mr Fox is a spiv – a dealer in second-hand cars and
black-market food, a man skilled in bending the law. When
Caroline Seymore and her young daughter Jenny are
deserted at the beginning of World War II, he offers them a
roof over their heads, advice on evading creditors and a
shared – if dubious – future. . . .

'I recommend it for its hilariously accurate descriptions of
war . . . Barbara Comyns had me by the throat in that
chokey state between laughter and tears given us by all too
few writers'
Mary Wesley, London Daily News

'An extremely funny book'
Literary Review

'It has great charm'
The Times

'I enjoyed her story . . . for its innocence, its
straightforwardness, its charming lack of guile'
Nina Bawden, Daily Telegraph

'Delicate poignancy wrapped up in beautifully elegant
prose'
Women's Review

'A minor classic . . . hunt down *Mr Fox* forthwith for its
peerless evocation of an era'
Daily Mail

MAUREEN DUFFY

CHANGE

'[Maureen Duffy] shows at once broad and deep
understanding of what the war of 1939–45 meant for
ordinary English men and women, both in and out of
uniform: a delight to read.'
M. R. D. Foot

To different people in Britain in 1939 the coming of war
meant different things. To Hilary at a London grammar
school it meant her father joining the Home Guard and
later, her school moving to the country and reaching
adulthood in a dangerous and exciting world. To Alan it
meant learning to fly and risk his life nightly, as well as
trying to respond with his poetry to the challenges of new
experience. To Daphne it meant separation from her army
officer husband and making a new life for herself as an
ambulance driver in the Blitz . . .

'It's as if our parents' and grandparents' treasured
photograph albums had been tossed in the air and their
snapshots, frozen moments in time, had landed heaped and
entwined. Maureen Duffy has picked through these
fragments of life and fitted them into the mosaic of
Change.'
Time Out

'In *Change* Maureen Duffy demonstrates her ability to be
simultaneously involved and yet distanced. It is this
merging of the implicated and prophetic voice that makes
her writing continually and unpredictably challenging.'
Fiction Magazine

'The telling is vivid, very readable.'
Financial Times

'An experienced, prolific novelist; nothing she writes
can fail.'
Daily Telegraph

Women's Writing from Methuen

While every effort is made to keep prices low, it is sometimes necessary to increase prices at short notice. Methuen Paperbacks reserves the right to show new retail prices on covers which may differ from those previously advertised in the text or elsewhere.

The prices shown below were correct at the time of going to press.

☐ 413 41360 8	**Oroonoko and Other Stories**	Aphra Behn	£3.95
☐ 413 41840 5	**Men Have all the Fun**	Gwynneth Branfoot	£3.95
☐ 413 59180 8	**The Juniper Tree**	Barbara Comyns	£3.50
☐ 413 40490 0	**Nothing Natural**	Jenny Diski	£2.50
☐ 413 54660 8	**Londoners**	Maureen Duffy	£2.95
☐ 413 60470 5	**I Want To Go To Moscow**	Maureen Duffy	£3.50
☐ 413 57930 1	**Here Today**	Zoë Fairbairns	£1.95
☐ 413 57550 0	**The Border**	Elaine Feinstein	£2.95
☐ 413 54630 6	**The Riding Mistress**	Harriett Gilbert	£2.95
☐ 413 59940 X	**Necessary Treasons**	Maeve Kelly	£3.95
☐ 413 60230 3	**Non-Combatants and Others**	Rose Macaulay	£3.95
☐ 413 57040 1	**Axioms**	Sheila MacLeod	£3.50
☐ 413 59750 4	**Daddy Was a Number Runner**	Louise Meriwether	£3.50
☐ 413 57940 9	**Movement**	Valerie Miner	£3.50
☐ 413 14010 5	**The Women of Brewster Place**	Gloria Naylor	£3.95
☐ 413 55230 6	**The Wild Girl**	Michèle Roberts	£2.95
☐ 413 42100 7	**Death of an Ex-Minister**	Nawal El Saadawi	£2.95
☐ 413 51970 8	**Sassafrass, Cypress & Indigo**	Ntozake Shange	£2.95
☐ 413 60100 5	**Broderie Anglaise**	Violet Trefusis	£3.50
☐ 413 14710 X	**The Women's Decameron**	Julia Voznesenskaya	£3.95
☐ 413 41830 8	**Prisons of Glass**	Elizabeth Wilson	£3.95

All these books are available at your bookshop or newsagent, or can be ordered direct from the publisher. Just tick the titles you want and fill in the form below.

Methuen Paperbacks, Cash Sales Department, PO Box 11, Falmouth, Cornwall TR10 109EN.

Please send cheque or postal order, no currency, for purchase price quoted and allow the following for postage and packing:

UK	62p for the first book, 22p for the second book and 14p for each additional book ordered to a maximum charge of £1.75.
BFPO and Eire	62p for the first book, 22p for the second book and 14p for each next seven books, thereafter 8p per book.
Overseas Customers	£1.64 for the first book plus 25p per copy for each additional book.

NAME (Block Letters) ....

ADDRESS..

....